An RMHFW publication.

First published on Amazon Kindle 2021.

Second edition published 2024.

This edition was published in 2026.

Breakout Road © Russell Martin Holdaway 2021.

https://www.russellmholdawayfreelancewriter.com/home

For Mum, Shirley Richardson, who never lost faith
in my writing. You are missed.

29/07/2020.

Emerald.

Queensland.

1605.

Senior Constable Melanie Hobson looked around the street before climbing into her Divisional four-wheel drive. Everything looked peaceful around the manicured lawns of the closely packed modern houses. Her eyes returned to the house she had just left, jaw tight. This was the third Peeping Tom she had had in this area this month. Turning the engine on, she lowered her mask and took a moment to enjoy the feel of the air-conditioning blowing on her face. It was a hot day, and the cool air was bliss. With a sigh, she reached for the mic mounted on her shoulder. Depressing the button, she spoke.

"Five-eight-six to control, are you receiving over?"

There was a pause before a female voice crackled back at her.

"Control receiving 586, over."

"Can you call all units in or around the Emerald Flats estate to be on the lookout for a Caucasian male with dark hair and approximately mid to late twenties? Blue flannel shirt. Jeans. About 180cm tall. If they see him, he's a POI for peeping and prying on the Emeralds Flats estate. Over."

The clipped voice repeated the details back to her.

"That's an affirmative. 586 out."

Replacing her mask, Hobson looked around before dropping the four-by-four into gear. These reports were beginning to

3

come in more often. The peeper was becoming brazen. Hobson was starting to worry. Glancing at the clock on the large screen fixed onto the dash, she pulled the vehicle smoothly onto the road. She had twenty-five minutes before O'Hare knocked off at the golf course. There was time to do a quick cruise around the estate. Looking from left to right, eyes taking in everything, she turned out of the street.

Michael O'Hare crouched, bringing himself down to examine the sand of the bunker at the thirteenth hole. Sweat trickled down his face, and his grimy blue denim work shirt clung to him as he looked across the sand. He ran his hand through his damp hair, and his mullet now clung to his head. He smiled with satisfaction. The evenness of the trap was a work of art. Glancing at the sun, he removed his hat and wiped the sweat from his forehead. Although the temperature had maxed out at about three o'clock, it was still hot. But it was a dry heat, so at least it was comfortable. Glancing at his watch, he grinned. It *was* four-thirty, well past knockoff time. As of thirty minutes ago, he had finished work. Best of all, it was payday. He had to admit that payday was no longer as much fun as it used to be. Everything was closed due to COVID-19 restrictions, limiting opportunities for fun and entertainment. Outside venues, such as the golf courses and parks, were the only places open. Still, payday it was. It was not just about money; he would not claim the overtime he had just worked. He disliked leaving a job half done. It would have bothered him all night, knowing that the sand trap was not smooth. Stretching, he was easing the knots out of his muscles when his phone buzzed. The Grouplink tone beeped. Mick pulled it out.

How was your day, young man?

Mick grinned. Con seemed to spend a lot of time in the 4x4 social group. At first, it had seemed odd to Mick that Con was so active on the Grouplink, but then he learned the man was from a seaside suburb around Melbourne. Victorian restrictions were so tight that Mick figured Con had little else to do. The man was living his freedom vicariously through others on Grouplink. Mick was happy to indulge his virtual mentor; it gave him a sense that he was helping the lonely man.

Good Sensai. Hard yakka on a hot day, so a bit tired.

Makes showers good, but. U?

Full on. Washing the washing. Hanging out the washing.

Waiting for the washing to dry. Watching the rain make it wet again.

The height of excitement.

Grinning, Mick replied.

I'm impressed, I didn't think you knew how

the machine worked. How's Marika?

There was a pause. Putting the phone away, Mick started walking away from the sand trap when it beeped again. He pulled it back out and flicked open the app.

How did the lights work out?

Mick grinned. He recently bought lights from Con. After having them painted to match *the Mutant's* olive drab, he had spent the last three evenings installing them across his roof rack. He had finished the wiring last night.

Great. Worth the money thanx.

U sure u don't want more? I feel like I ripped U off.

All good young man. They went to a good home.

You're not trying to groom me? Lol

No. My wife wouldn't stand for it.

She kept saying the house was too crowded

with me and the cat.

Mick smiled. It was the first time in a while that Con had mentioned his wife.

I'm taking the Mutant out tonight. Proper test. I'll flick you a pic.

I look forward to seeing it If I'm still here.

How's sunny Frankston?

There was a pause, and Mick started to put his phone away again when it pinged.

Can't say for sure. Lockdown.

All I can say is the garden is watered and I'm cold.

How's Emerald?

Mick laughed.

Warm. Sunny. With a nice SW breeze.

Good for you. I'll leave you to it for now.

Time to take my pills, and pee. Never get old young 'un.

It's lonely. You take so many pills you sound like a child's rattle. And you are always peeing.

Mick grinned. He'd seen photos of Con on Grouplink, leaning casually against his Land Cruiser 75, cigarette in his hand with a vista of mountains behind. He was kicking on in years, true, but looked strong as a Mallee Bull, his olive complexion belaying his age. Mick tapped a reply.

As you like to say, you are only as old as the woman you feel.

I need to ask you at some point about winches.

Mine was second-hand and can be a bit dodgy.

I've saved money and can afford to replace it.

Thanks again, Sensei. Take care.

And you. Be good or be good at it.

Sensai was the nickname Mick gave his off-roading mentor, whose advice had helped Mick prioritise the modifications of *the Mutant*. This time, Mick waited a few more moments. Con sometimes replied with a last nugget of advice. Disappointed when none came, Mick closed the app and slid his phone into the thigh pocket of his navy work pants. He only knew the man from the forum, but Con's Grouplinking *had* seemed a bit down lately. Mick could not put his finger on how, but Con did not seem as jovial as he used to. Maybe it was a combination of age and the isolation of the lockdowns. It could not be easy for Victorians, stuck in a house with one another. Mick resolved to initiate messages with the man rather than just answering them. As for the lights? When they had arrived two weeks ago, he had been expecting dented hand-me-downs at the price Con had asked. Instead, he received four state-of-the-art, still-in-the-box Bushranger Nighthawk VLI 9 series driving lights. When he had queried it, Con insisted there was no mistake. He simply did not need them as he had thought he would when he bought them. Although he felt a ripple of guilt about accepting such a generous offer, Mick was not about to complain. He wondered again if, somehow, he had taken advantage of Con but could not see how. It wasn't as if he knew Con had them in a shed. He hadn't approached Con directly. He asked in the forum if anyone had any old driving lights kicking around. His thoughts were interrupted by a harsh voice, bringing him back to reality.

"C'mon, fucknuts, we'll be late. We gotta meet the girls, and I gotta have a shower to wash this crap out of my hair."

Mick looked absently up. In his best clothes, Jack Higgins somehow managed to look untidy. He looked well out of place in the manicured surroundings, dressed in his work dungarees and green flannel shirt. His mullet of black curly hair was matted with the day's dirt and grime. Leaves and twigs stuck out from under his collar, and streaks of dirty sweat ran down his dark face.

"I've stood here for fifteen minutes while you caress that sand. It's lovely. Perfect. You could bounce a fuckin coin off it."

He turned, heading away from the bunker's edge, calling over his shoulder. "C'mon, the ladies await."

"All right. Chill, dude, we've got time," grinned Mick as he took one last look at his work. He turned and headed up the slope to Jack, using his rake as a staff. He stopped short at the sight of Jack, who was now waiting behind the driver's seat of the tool-laden golf buggy.

"Wait, wait, wait, wait, wait. You're not driving. Boss's orders after you drove the last two into the dam."

"Nah. It'll be fine. He *loves* you. And he can't sack *me*. I'm on a government scholarship. We're a package deal, you and me. I'm innocent by default when we hang together. Besides, he's working from home, so he won't know. Plus, I know where I went wrong those times. That second time wasn't all bad. You got to test the winch on the back of *the Mutant*. C'mon Mick. Live a little,"

Jack babbled with his characteristic grin. Mick had the impression Jack had been rehearsing this speech.

"Wipe that cocky grin off your face and fuck off out of the driver's seat. We don't need another mark against us," said Mick, sliding the rake into the back of the buggy. Jack was one of the best apprentices in their course, which was one of the reasons he was still employed, but it did not mean he was untouchable.

"Well...if you're gonna be a dick," Said Jack and pressed his foot on the accelerator. Mick yelled as the buggy lurched off, zipping across the green. It dipped down, passed a flag, and onto the track leading to the maintenance sheds.

"Come back, you dumb fu..ah, forget it."

Grinning, Mick began walking. For as long as he had known him, Jack had been impulsive, often joking that Mick had kept him out of jail. Some people called Jack a troublemaker, but Mick didn't see it that way. He was just full of life. No one worked harder in the Club than Jack; Mick just wished his mate would occasionally curb his impulsiveness. Jack had managed to get himself into *serious* trouble six months ago. He had been caught drag-racing his Dad's vintage HQ Monaro. Of course, it had to have been Hobson who caught him doing 160 km/h. Somehow, Jack had charmed the magistrate, who chalked it up to "the exuberance of youth".

Even so, Jack was now on a recognisance order. He needed to be careful. Mick walked across the green to the track a few hundred meters down, where Jack was waiting for him.

"C'mon fuck nuts," Jack's voice carried across the green, interrupting the swing of a couple of local businessmen. Mick had a feeling one of them was the mayor, but he couldn't say for sure. They glared disapprovingly.

Climbing into the buggy's passenger seat, his head started to bob as AC/DC played on the Bluetooth speaker Jack had strapped to the side of his lunch bag.

Mick said, "Look, I still don't know about tonight. What if we get caught? You're already on a recog? And I don't want to cause Mum anymore stress. She's drinkin' heaps lately. Now drive care-" he was cut off as the buggy lurched off spitting up grit.

"How many times, I gotta say. Trust me. Hobson won't even know we're out if we keep off the main roads and don't fire up your spotties near town. She'll stay tucked up in bed."

Mick thought about an old saying of his father's;

"If someone feels they have to say trust me, they expect to be mistrusted. Be careful."

A pang of resentment stabbed at Mick. His father had never said, *"Trust me."* And look how that ended.

"But-"

"Look, I've wanted to hook up with Josey since, like, Year Nine. I couldn't believe it when she answered my text. The least you could do is fake interest in her twin," Jack spared a sideways glance, "her *hot* twin. I mean, it's not like I'm askin' you to go with a pog."

"Look where you're driving! " Mick's voice ended in an unmanly screech as the buggy lurched around a bunker and drifted back onto the track. As Jack regained control, Mick shouted to be heard over the wind.

"I'd be leading her on. That's not right."

"Get over it. Jo wants to double date with her sis. You back out, Leanne backs out. Then Jo backs out. I then have another date with my hand tonight. You owe me this for...I dunno...something."

"But she's not my type."

"The year ten camp thing again. So, she doesn't like bugs. It was a *big* spider. Not all chicks have to dig camping. I mean, she's smart. She's gonna be a lawyer, for fuck's sake. I mean, there are worse types out there..." A sly grin broke across Jack's face. "Oh, I get it. I get it now. She's not Akina. Look, dude, I get it. Akina likes camping and knows fourbie engines like the back of her hand, and she's easy on the eye. But you and her? Brother, you're in the friend zone. Besties. Also, her old man'd crème you if he found you together. It'll never happen."

Mick sighed. Closing his eyes for a moment, he relished the air rushing on his face. He looked back at Jack.

"I know, man, but...she's so...so...Awesome," He finished. He knew he sounded lame, but it was how he felt.

"Awesome. Awesome?"

Mick gripped the side of the buggy as Jack nearly rolled it, rounding the corner onto the road leading to the maintenance sheds.

"Nah, man. You got it wrong." Jack continued leaning as the buggy steadied. "Hot. You mean hot. Chicks are hot. Mates are awesome. She's a mate. Trust me."

Mick winced as his stomach lurched, as the buggy shot over the rise of a green. There it was again. The 'trust me'.

"Then we're mates," Mick could not tell if the feeling in his gut was down to Jack's driving or what he said; either way, he resented Jack right then. Jack stared at Mick blankly.

"Mates?"

Mick pointed ahead. "Jack!"

"With a chick?"

"Look where you're going," Mick's voice rose slightly.

"I don't follow," Jack looked ahead and swerved the buggy, narrowly missing a tree. He dodged Mick's playful swat as he shot through the narrow storage shed doors, sliding the buggy to stop centimetres from the wall. Finally, letting go of the side of the buggy, Mick glared at Jack.

"Dickhead."

Jack grinned and hopped out.

After they put the buggy on charge and packed away their tools, they headed through the garage to the carpark.

"I don't get it. Why are you so intent on meeting Jo tonight anyway? I mean, it's not like chicks aren't lined up for you?"

Jack jumped out of the buggy.

"True. But chicks aren't Jo."

He hurried around to busy himself with cleaning the tools. That was when it hit Mick. *'Since Year Nine.'* He stopped short; this time, it was his turn to grin slyly.

"Wait. What? No!"

"What?"

Jack stopped a few steps ahead. He turned and seemed interested in a no-smoking sign over Mick's shoulder.

"That's lookin' tatty. I'll need to replace it," Jack's voice was too casual.

"Ah, no. Am I hearing this? Jack. The great stud. 'I'll never get tied to one chick,' Jack. *Jack the lad.* Could it be my best mate is in...love?"

A flickering light now caught Jack's attention.

"What? Nah? 'Course not. She's been on my-"

"...radar since Year Nine," Mick mimicked, "dude, when it comes to chicks, you've got an attention span of like...minutes. This is a crush. A four-year-"

"Three and a half," Jack's eyes had snapped onto Mick's.

"Whatever. A three-and-a-half-year crush. Fuck me. Dude. You are smitten. I see it now. All those field trips you were too cool for until you saw she was there. All those 'lame dances' you suddenly suited up for. Lit studies in Year Ten?"

"Yeah, that was a mistake." Jack struck a dramatic pose, *"To be or not to be?* What the fuck is that about? We weren't even in the same class."

"Not even the same year."

"Stupid accelerated classes. Why does she want to finish school a year ahead?"

Mick looked at his friend. He stepped forward and clutched Jack by the shoulders, gazing into the dark eyes. "What I'm saying to you, Maverick, is I'm here. I'm your wingman. You need me tonight; I got your back. I'll take this for the team."

There was immense relief on Jack's face.

"Cheers, man. I owe you one. Don't mess this up for me, though."

"But Jo? I mean, no one saw that coming."

They turned and carried on to the car park.

"Dude. I don't get it either. But she and me have been clicking on Grouplink. Turns out she's had a thing for me, too. But her Dad was always like. "No". She thought it was...you know...cause I'm black. Turns out it was 'cause he had to defend me so much. In court. Seems Dads don't like that in future boyfriends. A month back, he was like, 'I've not seen Jack in court. Is he okay?' and she's like 'he's kept a steady job since the end of year ten. He's got plans for the future.' And he's like. 'Really?' She's like, 'Yeah...can we date?'. He's like, 'Well, the rest of his family's decent, hard-working. Looks like Jack's heading that way; if he can keep his nose clean, then okay.' So here we are. Dude, I think this is it. I think I might settle for a bit. You know. Go steady. I *really* like her. The thing is, with her heading to Brisbane next year to go to uni, we don't have much time."

"And how do you think 'keeping our noses clean' is helped by breaking lockdown?" said Mick mildly.

Jack shrugged.

"That's why I need you there. You and Leanne will make us innocent by association. Leanne's following in her dad's shoes. Lawyering. And you ooze good guy."

Mick shook his head. One more offence and Jack would be in deep trouble. He did not seem to understand this.

"If we get caught, we are done. But you'll be *well done.* I'm serious. We'll have to kiss J&M Gardens goodbye."

Jack looked at him, "You'll find another business partner. CAN I RELY ON YOU?"

Realising Jack was not in the mood for sense, Mick shrugged. "I'll do my best."

Jack paused, looking serious. He reached out his hand. Mick took it, and they hugged. Jack grabbed the back of Mick's head and looked firmly into his face.

"I haven't forgotten our plan. It's just...I can't stay cooped up all the time. I need to get out. We *will* launch J&M. In eighteen more months, we will be our own bosses. Okay. Brother from another mother."

Mick nodded and returned the hug. Then Jack stepped back and slapped Mick's face. Mick stumbled under the blow. With a grin, Jack said, "Just don't get so caught up on Akina that you forget to have a good time tonight."

"I'll do my best," Laughed Mick, rubbing his face. "C'mon. We're done here. Home time."

Jack gave a whoop as they started to move around, switching off lights.

Mick forced open the side door, and they winced momentarily as they stepped into the sun. He felt a slight smile tug at his mouth as he looked across the car park at the vehicle he had dubbed *the Mutant*. The exact make of her was difficult to determine at a glance. She was an imported vehicle with so many add-ons and modifications that her original lines were obscured entirely. He had painted *The Mutant* a drab olive green, and he had let Jack finish it off with a painting of a gap-toothed zombie Kangaroo on the bonnet. The door squeaked as he climbed into the driver's seat. The smell of vinyl and oil tickled his nose. His phone bleeped. Mick pulled it out. It was a message from Con.

Lockdown extended in Vic. The isolation continues.

"Ah fuck," grunted Mick. Queensland had been under some restrictions, but Victoria was now in its fifth or sixth lockdown.

Sorry to hear that. If it makes you feel better, we are in the same boat.

Jack pulled his Patrol up next to him. He yelled to be heard over the rumbling motor.

"Remember, dude, seven-thirty. The Botanical Gardens. Under the bridge."

Mick grinned. "Yeah, I know."

Jack looked at the phone in Mick's hand.

"Hope that's not a date with Akina. I'm relying on you."

"Nah. It's Con. Vic's just extended lockdown again."

Jack winced.

"Poor fuckers. Remember, seven-thirty."

Jack's Patrol lurched away with a roar, peppering *the Mutant* with grit as he headed off along the golf course's drive.

Mick grinned as he turned the key. The powerful V8 turned over twice and then shuddered into life. A small red light flickered on the dashboard. After a few more seconds, a beep sounded as his phone connected, and AC/DC blasted out of the speakers.

"Bit thirsty, darlin'?" he said. His phone beeped again. It was Con.

You young'uns should be out having a life.

Mick switched his thread to Jack.

I gotta fuel up. U need anything?

Then, after a moment, he opened his thread to Con. Let the old guy hear some good news. With a grin, he typed,

I heard that. Up to mischief tonight. On a date.

Mick waited as the engine warmed. His phone beeped after a few moments.

Good to hear young man. LOL. Be good or be good at it.

Mick grinned. His phone beeped again. Jack had replied.

Dude, u don't got time for Akina.

That message was almost immediately followed by the following;

Can u grab some dingas? I'm out. 😊

K. But do they stock mini water bombs at the servo?

You'll keep. Say hi to Akina for me.

Mick dropped the phone onto the passenger seat, looked into his rearview mirror, and slid the gearshift into reverse.

29/07/2020.

Emerald Golf Course.

1720.

In a cloud of acrid smoke, Mick eased *the Mutant* out of the parking spot and headed down the golf course's drive. He pressed a small button he had added to his steering wheel. AC/DC cut out, and a smooth female voice said,

"Bluetooth device one is connected, name please?"

"Call mum. Mobile." Mick said.

There was a moment of silence, and then the mute brrrp brrrp of the phone ringing.

"Hi, Mick," his mother, Tilda, sounded tired.

"On the way home. Need anything?"

"Nope. All good. Be quick. Dinner's nearly ready."

"Cool, see you in a bit. Put the kettle on."

He cut off Tilda's 'bye'. As always, anticipation began to flutter in his stomach when he was headed to his favourite service station. He worked through the gears and headed up the drive more sedately than Jack. At the gate of the golf club, his phone buzzed again. Ignoring it, Mick waited for the traffic to clear before pulling out. He could feel his dopey grin as he headed down the road toward the workshop area of town. He was still grinning five minutes later as he turned off the highway. The engine purred as he cruised down a side street and turned into the forecourt of the old-fashioned mechanic/service station. Mick pulled up next to the vintage bowser, put the hand brake on, turned off the motor and jumped out. Moving down the side of *the Mutant,* he opened the fuel cap. Lifting the pump, he inserted the petrol nozzle, pulled the lever and started pumping, his head bobbing to the rhythmic ticking of the bowser. Then he caught sight of the all-too-familiar Police Divisional Land Cruiser as it slid by. Behind the wheel sat Senior Constable Melanie Hobson, gazing coolly around as she drove slowly past. Her face was unreadable behind the ever-present reflective sunglasses and police-issued N95 mask. Her hat perched smartly on her immaculately combed head; she caught a second glance at the sight of *the Mutant* before scanning the area around. Mick's head stopped bobbing at the sight of the police cruiser, watching warily as it pulled out of sight. His head began bobbing again. Mel...*Constable Hobson* Mick corrected himself; she had not been Mel for long. Constable Hobson always made him feel like he was breaking the law when he saw her. Why was she everywhere he was? He remembered when he used to think of her as a sort of big sister. That was a long time ago. Things had changed. His thoughts were cut as the pump kicked in his hand. He pulled the nozzle back a few moments and started the flow again. It ran for a few more seconds before kicking again, the petrol gurgling into the tank. He replaced the pump and screwed in the cap before heading in to pay. Pushing open the reflective glass door, he walked into the cool service area. Mick breathed in deeply, allowing nostalgia to wash over him as the tantalising sweet aroma of lollies, overcooked meat pies, and dried potato scallops enveloped him. In the background, he could hear a transistor radio relaying the latest press release from the premier's office.

"...are still to be worn in Southeast Queensland. Following new local cases, this will continue for another seven days as a precaution.

Then, a woman's voice.

"It's so important to wear a mask, and I genuinely believe they are stopping the spread into the community. They do more than protect you. They also remind you to be cautious, keep 1.5m away from another person, and get tested if you have symptoms. They are an excellent strategy, so we must continue wearing them for an extra week."

Tuning the radio out, Mick walked between the rows of convenience items. He had made this walk nearly every day since he first met Akina Sato in year seven. Even as a kid, finding excuses to stop by, hoping to see her after school. He always felt his pulse pound in his throat, his mouth dry. Two years ago, he had only been interested in talking 4x4s with her. But his feelings towards Akina had changed drastically over the past two years as the pair developed through their teens. He had long reconciled that he would be in, as Jack had put it, the 'friend zone'. Nothing serious would ever happen between them, but he always hoped. This was one time he hoped he would not see Akina sitting at the cashier's desk as he peeked between the bags of chips. With some relief, he noted it was unattended. He moved to where the condoms were kept, hanging above the shelves of soaps, toothpaste and feminine hygiene products. He grabbed a packet of "Ribbed X-iters" and walked to the counter, stopping short as he caught sight of Akina. She seemed to have materialised on the seat behind the counter. Gazing at her phone, she appeared not to have noticed him. She looked up and gave him that dazzling smile, her face framed by freshly combed, short black hair. If he had not been so distracted, Mick might have noted that the hair was not tousled, that her jade green blouse's top buttons were undone, and the gloss on her lips was fresh. But it was her eyes that held him. Since they met in year seven, he had been drawn by her eyes. Her dark, almond-shaped eyes seemed to remove him from the world. They shone bright with life and intelligence, but when angered, would harden like obsidian. When she wore a face mask, he found her eyes more alluring. But now her mask was pulled down so he could see her dazzling smile. He found himself gazing into those warm brown eyes. His mouth suddenly desiccated. He forgot how to speak. For a moment, he forgot why he was there. He had been drawn into a dream. They were sitting on a rug on a beach up north. *The Mutant's* rooftop tent was set up, and a fish he had caught was cooking over a small fire. They hugged, gazing out at the orange ocean as the sun set. Then they looked into each other's eyes; she took his cheek and leaned in and-

"Sorry, what?" he stammered, the ocean disappearing. The sunset disappeared, too. The roar of the waves faded into the sound of blood rushing through his ears.

"Have you got the new lights up?" Akina repeated slowly, dragging him reluctantly back to the here and now. Her interest was genuine. She had helped him with most of the mods on his rig, at times taking charge. In some ways, she knew *the Mutant* better than he did. She had grown up around 4x4s. Her father owned the service station and mechanical workshop. He had always encouraged his daughter to tinker with engines, initially to ensure that mechanics could not take advantage of her later on. However, as her interest increased, it became how the man bonded with his daughter. Jack's heart leapt into his throat.

"Huh?"

"New lights…Look good…Very shiny," She repeated as if speaking to a six-year-old, her eyes smiling.

"Er, thanks," he croaked, feeling his face redden. He had become suddenly *very* aware of the condoms in his hand. He looked for somewhere to dump them discreetly, but realised there was nowhere. Kicking himself for coming here, he placed them on the counter. Akina's eyes, so warm when he entered the shop, were suddenly obsidian.

"Oh. Going on a date, stud?"

"Er, they're not for me. They're for Jack."

"Jack?"

Mick nodded.

"Your mate. From school. Who put washing detergent in the fountain during Australia Day?" Her voice was now flat.

"Yeah. He has a date tonight. He asked me to pick some up for him. I guess he's feelin' lucky. I'm wingman. Not that I want to be. But mates gotta stick together." He ended with a weak chuckle.

"Really? Not that you want to?" she arched an eyebrow, her voice clipped as if biting off each word. She buttoned up her Jade-coloured blouse.

Turning crimson, Mick nodded furiously. He gestured to the condoms.

"He's out."

"Jack," She pulled the mask up to her face.

"Yeah."

'Your best mate."

"Yeah?"

Mick sensed danger.

"With Josey Wright. Right?"

"How'd you…"

Akina gave Mick a flat look.

"Jack was in here five minutes before you. Two potato scallops. 'A packet of dingers,' as he put it. No fuel. He was very pleased with himself. 'Feeling lucky,' he said."

Mick closed his eyes, his face flushing red. He vowed to hurt Jack for this.

"$116.86," said Akina.

He handed $120 over; she slapped his change on the counter.

"I hope your night goes well. Oh, and next time…" Her voice was clipped as she pointed to the sign that said,

"NO MASK NO SERVICE".

Realising he had left his mask in the car, Mick nodded and left the shop. His mind raced as he strode angrily across the forecourt to his rig.

"I'm going to kill him. I might actually fucking kill him," He muttered as he ripped open the squeaking door and put his right foot on the running plate. He gripped the handle above the door, ready to swing into the ute. He paused a moment as his eyes rested on his phone, suddenly realising he could show Akina Jack's message. A voice cut across his thoughts.

"Michael O'Hare. Where is your mask?"

Mick froze, closing his eyes slowly. Hobson had doubled back. Stepping down, he turned and looked up at the tall, lean woman before him.

"Yeah. Er. It's in my er…"

"No good there," She said.

"Sorry."

Hobson grabbed Mick and pushed him against the side of his truck. She looked down into his eyes, his face reflected in her sunglasses. Between the mirrored shades and the blue mask she wore, he could not make out much of her tanned face.

"Say that to your Mum as she's on her deathbed because you brought it home. Or to the cute little biscuit in there, you just infected."

"Huh?" Mick was confused now. "Oh. Right."

"How is she?"

He gestured with a limp hand at the service station.

"Angry, we've had-"

"Your Mum dip shit."

"Oh. She's good. She keeps her mouth coated with vodka to kill germs, so…you know."

Hobson ignored the comment.

"She's a good woman, Mick. Treat her with respect. She's been through a lot."

Hobson had not let go of his arm. He gave it a shake, it had starting to tingle.

"Whereas it's been a cruise for me. I'll treat her like a queen. Can I go now?"

Pins and needles enveloped his hand as Hobson let go. She cast her eyes over the truck.

"New lights, eh?"

"Yes. They have covers on."

"I see that. Lift legal?"

"You know it is."

"Those tyres are barely legal."

Mick gritted his teeth.

"I know. She's booked in for a refit at Berg's next week. I can show you the confirmation text."

Hobson shook her head.

"No need. You know there's a lockdown? You might have heard it in the media. Essential travel only? Distance limits. Masks. Businesses closed? Do you want a fine? Jail?"

Mick nodded. Frowned. Then shook his head.

"What are those for then?"

Hobson gestured to the condoms in his hand.

"Smuggling drugs."

His head rang as Hobson smacked the side of his head. She leaned forward.

"You and your mate better watch yourselves. I'm on the road tonight. I'll be watching for your...rig."

He could not see, but Mick had the sense that the last word was uttered with a curled lip.

Hobson turned and stalked back to the police cruiser. She climbed in and started the motor. She sat. Waiting. Watching. Her Cruiser's engine growling. Mick climbed into *the Mutant* and turned the key. The motor started with a belch of smoke, and he pulled out of the concourse. All the way home, he saw the police cruiser no more than two cars behind. Mick ignored his phone for the rest of the drive.

Melanie Hobson burst through the doors of the pool hall and sprinted across the road towards the taxi ranks. Behind her, she heard the whoops of the excited boys, three of them, running after her.

"C'mon dyke, we'll teach you to like men," Gasped one. Mel guessed it was Franco.

She glared back. Franco stumbled but kept running. The distance separating them was lengthening. Recognising her from school, the boys had taken an interest in her, inhibitions lifted by the grog the pool hall owner had sold them. The barman had known they were school-aged. He did not care. Mel had gone by herself to shoot some pool. It helped her to relax when her parents argued. Kept her away when things turned physical. Mel would not know who would hit who first, but they would both have bruises when she got home. At night, she would generally avoid the pool hall. It had a reputation, well-deserved. Today, she had decided to stop hiding.

"Yeah. Slow down. We'll make you smile," guffawed one of Franco's friends. Probably Ben. The three of them were year elevens and were not the crowd a year nine girl in her right mind would hang with. Mel was starting to breathe heavily, but at least she was putting distance between them. They were not fit at the best of times, but as drunk smokers, they were hopeless. Allowing herself a smile, Mel eased her pace a little. Stamina would get her out of this one as easily as speed. She turned up in the alley behind the shops. It was dark and smelled of stale beer and urine. Through it, she would loop back to the street that would take her home. About halfway down the graffiti-lined alley, she realised her mistake. A gate had been closed, preventing access to the back of the jewellers. Generally, she passed by here during the day. It was open. She had not even been aware there was a gate there until now.

"Damn," She hissed. She spun and sprinted back up the alley; the three boys rounded into it, coming to a surprised stop. Looking up the alley, Franco put it together and grinned lopsidedly.

"Hey, fellas...she's changed her mind."

Mel turned and sprinted back up the alley, propelled by legs like pistons up the wire mesh. She gripped the top of the gate, but her feet slipped. She hung for a moment, gasping, before using core strength to swing herself up. She looped her left leg over the top. A firm hand gripped her right ankle.

"Not so fast, darlin'," Laughed Ben. The least drunk of the three, he was also the tallest. He gave a couple of hard tugs, and she toppled back, winding herself as she landed heavily on the ground. She felt the left leg of her jeans catch on a wire and tear. Immediately, four firm hands picked her up and pressed her against the gate wire.

"Well," Franco breathed heavily, bent over slightly, his hand on his side. A faint wheeze was audible with his breath, which reeked of rum and pot. "You like to play hard to get."

He wiped the blood away from a nose which was now clearly broken thanks to Mel's elbow. Ben's eye was puffing up nicely, and Jeremy's lip was swelling up a treat. This gave Hobson a little satisfaction. She had put up a fight at the pool hall. She would have preferred it if the pool hall owner had helped rather than telling them to take it outside. It was Jeremy and Ben who had hold of her. Franco leaned in; she turned her face away from his fetid breath. He took her chin and turned her face to look into her clear blue eyes. His dark eyes were unfocused.

"Leave me alone, asshole," She spat.

Wiping her saliva from his cheek, he looked at his two friends. He made a clicking sound like a mother trying to settle an upset child. He straightened and slid his hand over her cheek.

"You looked lonely there by yourself. We just wanted to buy you a drink. Shoot some pool. But no. You're too good for us. Stop wiggling."

He gave her cheek a light slap.

"They get harder."

"I'll call the cops."

Franco laughed.

"Who'll believe you? Trash. A bitch from the estates. Versus me. *My* Dad. A respected and-"

A voice cut across the rant. A bright light sliced down the alley, lighting them all up.

"What goes on here then?"

The hands let go as the three boys spun. Mel dropped to her knees. All four of them winced in the torch's brightness.

Franco paused a moment, his addled brain bringing it together before he grinned.

"Ah, Constable O'Hare. How is your evening?"

"My evening was quiet. I had just filled my cup with coffee from my thermos flask. I was about to take a sip when I saw this young lady running down the road. I thought to myself, this is a funny time of night to be out for a jog. And...then...I...see...you. Three upstanding pillars of the community are running after her."

Jerry O'Hare began walking down the alley, his words in sync with his steps, crunching on the gravel and broken glass. His steps were the only sound in the alley. The Maglite's beam zeroed in on Franco. Unwavering. Franco's black, greased-back hair glistened in the light. He straightened to meet O'Hare's gaze.

O'Hare leaned in.

"And I think to meself 'not on my watch.' So I have to put my coffee down. This makes me cranky."

Franco's grin was smug as he looked at his friends.

"Look, how about you and I visit an ATM? I'll draw out...say...$150, I think, is the going price of a whor-"

The Maglite flashed as O'Hare drove it into the youth's stomach, dropping him to the ground, where he promptly vomited. Grimacing slightly, O'Hare bobbed down to Franco's level. The other two squared up to O'Hare.

"I wouldn't, lads," O'Hare snapped, glaring up at them. The two boys stepped back, suddenly uncertain.

"That's police brutality," said Ben, eyes wide.

O'Hare fixed Ben with a glare as Franco straightened up. Looking at the boys, he said, "Come on then. Have a go, lads. I'll expand your frame of reference about brutality."

His voice was quiet.

The two boys looked at each other. Then, keeping their backs pressed to the wall, edged past O'Hare and then ran. He turned back to Franco, who was getting to his feet.

"My father-"

"Is a powerful and hard-working man who would eviscerate you if he saw you tonight," O'Hare cut in through clenched teeth, "now fuck off before you really piss me off."

There was a moment when Mel thought Franco would take a swing at the tall constable. She hoped he would. Common sense prevailed, and the boy turned and limped back up the alley, nursing his stomach as he went. O'Hare turned his eye to her.

"I am Senior Constable Jerry O'Hare," he said formally. "Are you okay, Miss?"

Not trusting herself to speak, Mel nodded.

"What's your name, Miss?"

"Melanie Hobson."

Hobson said hesitantly. Her throat was dry, her voice cracked.

"Would you like to press charges, Miss Hobson?"

"Against *him*? Is there any point?"

O'Hare shrugged.

"Probably not. It couldn't hurt to piss him off, though, and his Dad'll creme him. C'mon, I'll drive you home."

They turned and headed back up the alley. Mel looked up to find O'Hare looking at her.

"You caused those injuries to the boys?"

Mel nodded.

"You must handle yourself well."

Mel felt herself smile.

"Dad has a boxing bag hung in the garage. He taught me a few things."

Her eyes darkened.

"They still caught me, but."

"That was dumb luck. You took a wrong turn. Life can be like that."

They stepped out of the alley. The brightly lit street jarring after the darkness of the alley. O'Hare gestured to the police car parked across the road.

"Why *are* you out this time of night?"

"My parents were fighting."

For some reason, Mel felt comfortable around this man. O'Hare nodded

"That's right. Hobson. I've paid you folks a visit in the past."

Mel shrugged. The lights on the police car flashed once as O'Hare unlocked it with the remote.

"Look, you know the YMCA?"

She nodded.

"There's a Judo club there. Meets three times a week, Monday evening 7-9, Wednesday evening 7-9 and Saturday morning 9-11. With some formal training, you could do well."

"Judo? Never heard of it."

"It's a martial art. You're trained to throw people around and tie them in knots. Not hurt them if you don't need to."

"I don't know."

"Nothing gives you confidence against bullies better than being able to kick their asses. You can't always rely on the world to fight the fight for you. With a bit of hard work on your part, you could look after yourself."

They reached the police car.

"Tell me more," Mel said. Intrigued.

Mick winced as he pulled into the drive behind his mother's 2005 Corolla. Things had not been good between them. He felt a pang of guilt at hoping she had pulled another double shift at the hospital. At least when she was working, she wasn't drinking. With a deep breath, he stepped onto the balcony. When he opened the door, the smell of spaghetti bolognese wafted into the humid air.

"Hello?" he called, kicking off his boots. His stomach rumbled as he stepped into the house.

"Hey, Mum, I'm home. Spag smells great," he called with forced levity. His gaze lingered on lighter patches on the hall wall, where the photos of his dad had once hung. The picture of his father's graduation from the police academy. A wedding photo, where a snap of his mother in a hospital bed cradling a newborn, Mick had been wedged. Mick smiled, remembering the goofy grin his Dad had as, with thumbs up, he leaned awkwardly across to be in the first family snap of the three of them. Tilda and Jerry, both pale, looking exhausted...but so happy. There were other patches, but those were the ones he missed. Mick swallowed, clenching his jaw, and his eyes hardened.

"Why did you leave you selfish..."

His stomach rumbled again, dragging him from his darker thoughts.

"Hey sweetie, how was work?"

Mick's head snapped right as his mother appeared in the kitchen doorway. She was still in her nursing scrubs, a tired smile on her gaunt face. He thought back to the photos. How happy she had looked. She had aged since Mick's Dad had left. Mick said nothing of the glass of red wine in her hand. What was the point? She was speaking again. He brushed past her, giving her a brief smile as he headed down the passage, dropping his work bag as he went.

"Well? Work? How was...are you even in there?"

"Tiring. I was on sand traps again," he said. "Jack drove a buggy today without crashing it. So that was a bonus."

As he moved through to his bedroom, he peeled off his sweat-drenched clothes, dropping them on the floor. Naked, he grabbed his wash bag and moved back into the hallway and into the bathroom. Tilda's voice came through the half-opened door.

"Me? Well, thanks for asking. It was tiring. We were down two again, which meant I had a patient load..."

He turned on the shower. As he waited for the steam to rise, he admired himself in the large rectangular mirror, bending his arm and flexing his bicep with an approving nod. He knew he had looks, but he wished he had the confidence Jack had. He was sure he and Akina would be together by now if he had. He barely heard his mother speaking.

"Meaning no one was coordinating discharges. KPI's out the window. Again."

There was a thump.

"Aw, Michael, please don't leave your stuff in the hall. I'm going to trip over it 'n break my neck."

"Sorry, Mum," He groaned, stepping into the shower.

"And dirty clothes go in the laundry."

"Yeah, I was gonna do that after my shower."

Leaning against the shower wall, Mick revelled in the water as it ran over the back of his head and down his tanned back. He drew a deep breath, sighing as he watched it turn beige, collecting the day's grime and carrying it, along with the day's stress, down the drain. It always felt good to watch. A symbolic washing away of the woes of work. He could feel the knots in his muscles beginning to loosen as he started scrubbing. For a short while, the cathartic flow of warm water drowned his mother's voice.

Thirty minutes later, Mick was at the table, slurping down spaghetti bolognese. He had to admit, ever since he was a kid, this had been his favourite meal. He reached across and grabbed more pizza cheese, tipping it over his steaming plate. He looked at Tilda, who was sitting opposite. After changing out of her scrubs, she wore a pink, tropical-print shirt and jeans. He grinned at Tilda, red sauce dripping down his chin. He glanced at the clock on the wall.

"Great spag, ma."

She looked at him speculatively as she dipped a chunk of garlic bread into the sauce. The silence between them thickened like glue. Mick looked at her, puzzled.

"You look nice, ma; what's the occasion?" he said between mouthfuls, hoping he had not missed another birthday.

"I figured as you were dressing up...I would."

Mick sensed she was waiting for something. He swallowed and gave a weak smile.

"Thanks?" he tried.

She nodded. Eyes narrowing. He hated this game. Why did women play this game? Where did they learn it? It was the silent game they played when they thought they knew what men were hiding. She was waiting for him to start babbling awkwardly, knowing he would let something slip. He filled the next minute, stuffing garlic bread and pasta into his mouth. He looked up again. Her gaze had not shifted.

"What?" he asked around a mouthful of pasta.

"You're also dressed smartly tonight."

"Thanks...again."

"You smell good, too."

"Er...weird, but thanks."

"Date?"

For the second time that day, Mick recognised the danger too late.

"Jack and I are gonna take *the Mutant* out to test the lights."

"Bit smartly dressed for that, aren't you?"

"Yeah, well, you keep saying I should take more pride in myself."

"You know there're restrictions. Last I checked, testing lights on heaps of junk is not one of the reasons to leave home."

Mick felt a flare of anger at the word junk.

"Yeah? We won't be in the same rig and..."

"That's your only button-up shirt."

"Yeah? Wait, what?"

He was sure he had others.

"Again. And don't lie. Date?"

"Look, ma-"

"Michael O'Hare, you know damn well the position it puts me in if you're caught."

Her Irish accent started to thicken as it always did when she was angry or drunk.

"Mum-"

She held up a finger, cutting him short.

"NO! I head the respiratory unit at the medical centre. You know how it looks when my son ignores the rules."

"But ma-"

"But nothing. I work all hours of the day under constant stress to put food on the table. I then get home and have to tidy up after you. And what do you do? Go on dates. And to cap it all off, you lie. To me."

"Wait up," Mick slammed his fork on the table. "You didn't gimmie a chance. I was going to tidy up after the shower, and why the FUCK *should* going on a date be illegal?"

"You mind your language, Michael O'Hare. And you are right. It is not fair. But right now, it *is* the law. It's about public safety. We all have to do our bit."

"Yeah, and that bit for my generation is to give up growing up."

"Don't be so damn selfish. If I'm not stuck in that fluorescently lit hell, I'm out sticking swabs up noses and down throats. I had someone vomit on me today. They had been eating tuna. Any idea what that's like? No. Of course not. You're too busy, spending thousands on that...that...thing out there-"

"What? Wait. Is *that* what's bothering you? I can't even have a fu...a hobby now? Is this about the lights? I told you what they cost."

Mick could feel his anger surging. His face flushed hot. A small voice told him to stand and leave. He ignored it.

"You think I'm lying about 'em. YOU WANNA SEE THE RECEIPT? Dad would've understood."

Tilda flinched. She took a deep breath and carried on in a calmer voice.

"You can have a hobby. Of course, you can. The least you could do is buy some things for the house."

"I pay board. I pay half the bills. Look, it's not my fault you don't *let* yourself have a life. Perhaps if you spent less on grog..."

Tilda's jaws clenched as she put her garlic bread down. Her movements were slow and deliberate.

"Listen here, young man-"

"No, enough listening. I didn't ask you to stop living after Dad left."

"He didn't *leave...*"

Mick cut across her, "I didn't tell you to stay in. All right, you needed time to adjust. I get that. So did I. But it's been two years now. It's not my fault you don't want to move one. Maybe if you'd lived a little, were a little less wound up, he would still be here."

Tilda was out of her chair, her green eyes blisteringly cold. "How dare you, you selfish little gob shite. You think dropping from two incomes to one is easy. Sure, he left us the house, but also the mortgage. D'you think of that? It'd go a long way to helping *me* have a life if you'd help pay that."

"You said that's what the board's for. Now you're saying you need more?" Mick was standing, breathing heavily.

"Yes. I want a life as well. I want a new car. A boyfriend. I want to go out and risk my life and thousands of dollars in fines for a quick knee tremble with some sleazy-"

Mick turned and headed for the door.

"I don't need to listen to this shit."

"Michael O'Hare, do not turn your back on me."

"Why not? Dad did. Perhaps you can take *my* photos down, too."

Jaw clenched, Mick pretended not to notice the silence as he walked out of the house.

Mick pulled *the Mutant* up under the rail bridge, as much into the shadow as he could manage, before switching off the engine and cutting out the radio. The car was suddenly silent. He looked across at Leanne, who was smiling back. Opening her mouth slightly, she ran her tongue along her bottom lip. Mick cleared his throat and looked out at Jack's patrol. Despite the shaky start at home, it had turned out to be a good night. Mick had met Jack a little way out of town. Jack had jumped into *the Mutant,* and for about forty minutes, they raced up and down the smooth highway, testing *the Mutant's* lights, whooping with glee as they lit the road for hundreds of meters ahead. They took photos, and Mick remembered to send one to Con, for which he received a thumbs up. Eventually, Jack got impatient and insisted they head back to meet the twins, who had climbed out of their bedroom windows and were waiting. They collected Jack's Patrol, picked up the twins, and headed to the botanical gardens. Jack, with Josey, had parked his Patrol brazenly in the middle of the carpark. Before the travel bans, these areas had been full of travellers stopping over for the night. Now the area was empty, and even though he knew *the Mutant* was hidden, Mick felt exposed. He sat for a few more moments, staring at the steering wheel, not wanting to meet Leanne's eye again. The engine's ticking was the only sound before Leanne spoke, her voice harsh in the silence.

"Shall we sit in the back?"

"It's not tidy back there. I keep chucking rubbish…"

Leanne smiled.

"I think I can take our minds off that...shall we?"

Startled, Mick looked at her for a moment. He swallowed. Then nodded. They climbed into the back seat, neither wanting to open the door to the cool night. After sweeping litter from the back seat onto the floor, Leanne wriggled out of her jacket and revealed a tight, tie-dye crop top. Mick tried not to stare, but it was apparent she was not wearing a bra. He leaned up against the door, putting distance between them, giving what he hoped was a casual smile. He caught his face reflected in the window behind Leanne. Seeing his uncomfortable grimace reflected, he let his face fall. For her part, Leanne was having none of it. She curled up next to him, grabbed his arm, and pulled it around her shoulder. He froze, not daring to move as his hand settled on her left breast.

"Such a cold night," She murmured.

He swallowed. Nodded. He swallowed again. How was he producing so much saliva?

"Makes you want to cuddle up to someone."

He nodded. The moment was awkward. For a minute, no one moved. No one spoke. Leanne sighed and looked out of the windows, which had started to steam up. She turned back to Mick. Her coy smile had returned.

"My bad, we must be warm. Perhaps we should slip out of these clothes."

Mick froze. His heart crashed like it was trying to blast out of his chest and escape the car itself. After an awkward moment, Leanne sat up. The sudden movement took Mick by surprise.

"Is everything okay?" he asked, his voice husky.

"That's what I was going to ask you?"

Mick's brow furrowed.

"I don't follow."

"Normally, at this point, guys are pawing at me, trying to...well, you know..."

Mick nodded. He knew. Well...guessed.

"But instead, there's so much tension here you could cut it with a knife."

Mick sighed.

"Look. Yeah. Okay," He sighed, choosing his words. He did not want to upset someone else today. "Look. I'm sorry. It's just...Don't get me wrong, you're hot and all," He waved his hand up and down, gesturing at her physique, accentuated by the tight light blue jeans and crop top. "I just don't want to get into a relationship."

He cut the sentence short, hoping she would not pick up on the unsaid "with you". He braced for the onslaught. But instead, Leanne sighed and gave him a sudden dazzling smile.

"You are soooo cute," She said after a pause. "Who wants a relationship? I am going to Uni in Brisbane next year to study law. The last thing I want is ties here."

She waved her hand, encompassing Emerald.

"Really?"

For a moment, her face tightened. She bit her lip before going on.

"Yes. Look. I'm just out for a bit of fun tonight," Her voice trembled slightly. "To escape from...everything. To feel something other than scared. Stressed. Alone."

Mick looked at her. At that moment, she seemed so vulnerable. All he wanted to do was comfort her.

"Look, there are other ways to feel closeness. I still feel close to Dad by working on *the Mutant*."

"I don't have a fourbie or the skills to work on one."

"True. But there's a bloke online. He gives me advice. Helps. Perhaps if you got a hobby, you might, you know, meet someone."

Leanne looked at him, head tilted as if not quite believing how this was going.

"I don't want to meet randoms online or fix trucks. I just want to feel...something. And tonight that something is with you."

Her coy smile returned as she slid her hand down his thigh and in between his legs. "And I can tell you feel the same. Why don't you try to live a little?"

Mick's mind was racing, his mouth suddenly dry. Was Leanne saying she just wanted a fling? She was vulnerable and upset. Was that right? Her hand began to rub slowly, and suddenly, he found it difficult to breathe. Vulnerable chicks were not his style. That was more Jack's way. He was suddenly aware he could not back any further from Leanne without jumping out of the ute, which he briefly considered. Part of him wanted to swat her hand away from his pelvis, but it did feel nice. Her hand slid up, and she began to unbuckle his belt deftly. Two hands feverishly unbuttoned his jeans. He looked down from her eyes, which had held his for the last two minutes. Her hands slid over his firm stomach and into his shorts. He looked up and found Leanne staring at him. Her intensity drew him in. There was now no vulnerability. Her eyes were large, and she knew exactly what she wanted. She leaned down, and suddenly, Mick did not care; this was not his style. She began kissing his stomach from the naval, moving down. She looked up at him.

"Mick, be honest," She whispered breathlessly. "Is this your first time?"

The question was so surprising that he did not consider lying. He nodded.

"That's okay," She said with a smouldering pout. "I'll be gentle."

Her voice was now husky as she leaned down into his lap. A light cut over Mick's shoulder into the cabin of *the Mutant*. A banging on the roof caused them both to jump. Leanne hit her head on the roof of *the Mutant* before squinting out the window.

"C'mon, you two out," Snapped an all too familiar voice.

"Ah, for fu-"

"I wouldn't finish that sentence, O'Hare," Hobson snapped as she grabbed the door handle. "OUT! C'MON. I don't have all night."

She yanked the door open. Mick, who had been leaning against the door, fell backwards. Leanne lunged to grab Mick but lost her balance and tumbled after him.

"Well, well, well. Micky O'Hare and our town's future legal eagle. Breaking lockdown laws is not a great start to a law career. I'm tippin' your journo sister is in there."

Hobson nodded toward Jack's gently rocking Patrol as Leanne, dusting herself off, got to her feet. With a frown, she reached down and tugged Mick's arm, prompting him to do the same. Turning her attention back to Hobson, she held her chin high and said,

"Harassment is not a great activity for a police officer."

Hobson paused. Mick could not see through the sunglasses and mask, but she seemed taken aback.

"What was that twinkles?" she asked.

Mick could hear the sneer under the mask. Leanne cleared her throat. She was used to debates.

"Well. Mick took great pains to park away from the entrance to conceal *the Mutant*. Whereas Jack, with his characteristic brazenness, has parked in plain view. This means you either ignored Jack's 4x4 or didn't see it. This means either one;" She held her forefinger or her right hand up. "You had a specific target or two." She held up her second finger. "You are terrible at your job. I ask myself, which is it? It is well known throughout Emerald that you are perceptive and notice EVERYTHING. So, I ask myself, please let me finish Senior Constable."

Leanne held up her hand as Hobson looked about to interrupt.

"I propose, therefore, that you have a specific target in Mick. I wonder what the Ethical Standards Command would think of such an experienced officer, a senior constable, harassing a 17-year-old in these trying times? Perhaps my 'journo sister' can write an article for the school news web page."

Mick stared at this last line, delivered by Leanne's characteristic raised eyebrow, as used during debates in class. Shaking her head, Hobson gestured to her police cruiser.

"Just get into my car, will you? I'm taking you home."

Leanne grabbed her coat and put it on. Then, with an arched eyebrow directed at Hobson, she turned to Mick. She leaned in, giving him a lingering kiss, and in a low voice, said.

"I suggest you button up."

Stepping back, she said more loudly.

"We will pick this up later."

As Leanne moved across the carpark, the meaning of her words sank in. He suddenly realised his jeans were undone, and he was exposed to the world. He hurriedly put himself away and buttoned up, suddenly realising his crotch was illuminated by Hobson's Maglite. He looked back at Leanne, who gave a small wave as she climbed into the back of the police car, closing the door.

"Must be the personality that attracts them. Though it *is* a cold night, I s'pose."

"What the fuck's your problem, Mel?"

"Problem? Me? Look here, kid; *I* should book the pair of you for public indecency, breaching restrictions, and for her...poor taste."

"True? Why don't you?"

"Because, you selfish little prick, your mother has enough on her plate." Hobson sighed, taking a moment to breathe.

"Look, your Dad and I were partners for five years, friends longer. He pulled me away from what would have been a bad life. I owe your family this much."

"Ah fuck off, he was piss weak and couldn't take the-"

This time, it was not a slap but a punch. Mick doubled over, clutching his stomach. He sank to the ground, coughing. Hobson grabbed him, pulling him to his feet and pushing back against the *Mutant*. She pulled down her mask and leaned in close to Mick's ear. Mouth barely moving, she snarled,

"Listen here, you entitled little ingrate. Your father was many things, but he was never weak. I ever hear you say otherwise..." Hobson left the threat hanging. "Just fuck off home, will you."

She turned and stalked back to her cruiser, stopping briefly by Jack's patrol to rap on the window.

"Nights over, you two. Wrap things up. Don't be here when I come back, Jack, or you'll be in breach of your bond."

Jack's bewildered face popped up in the window to watch Hobson walk away as two hands grabbed his face and pulled him back down. The patrol started rocking again.

Mick stood doubled over for a few more seconds, recovering his breath. Then he straightened, rubbing his gut. He saw Leanne fighting with the door handle, trying to get out of the car. As she climbed into the cruiser, Hobson snapped tiredly.

"Child locks dip shit. Put the seatbelt on."

Hobson said as she opened the door.

"I saw all of-" Leanne's voice was cut off as Hobson slammed the door. The SUV started up and rolled towards the entrance to the car park, pausing before pulling onto the road to head into town. Mick looked over to Jack's Patrol, which was still rocking, windows fogged.

His breath formed a cloud as he breathed a quiet "BooYah" At his friend.

His phone beeped. It was Con.

How was your night?

Fizzer. Cops caught us. Yours?

I got to speak to the kids. Say a decent goodbye.

Hug your mother. She won't be around forever.

Mick glared irritably at the phone. Why was everyone so worried about his Mum? Why can't someone tell *her* to treat *him* right? He replied.

Will do. Good night.

Goodbye.

Mick looked for a moment. Something was not right. Then it struck him: "Goodbye." Not "be good, or be good at it." He shook his head, too tired to care. He started his car and headed home.

30/07/2020.

Emerald.

0500.

The tune began gently. A relaxing melody, accompanied by quiet piano, rhythmic and settling. More melodies layered over the piano; the longer they were left, the louder they got. Eventually, they cut into Mel's dreams, waking her. With a groan, she squeezed her eyes tighter, trying to ignore the persistent, rolling tune.

"Shut that damn thing up," Naomi's voice, a soft, tired whisper floated from under the sheets next to her.

Mel's eyes opened. She had forgotten Naomi had stayed over. She reached across, cancelling the alarm, before rolling over and enveloping Naomi with a tender embrace. Sharing a final few moments of warmth, Mel breathed deeply, taking in the aroma of sweat with the hint of aviation fuel. Their relationship was young and tender. Still growing. She wondered again how Naomi felt about keeping it secret. Mel wanted it that way until they were sure what their relationship was. It had not been so long ago that they had just been meeting for coffee. Testing the waters before revealing their feelings for each other. Trust had been an issue. Naomi, because of her experiences in the US Marines. Mel, because of her experiences in a small town, in a masculine job. Mel knew the vast majority of Emerald would not care who she slept with. The small minority who did would either spruke their relationship in some virtue signalling symbolism, or deride it in some moralistic rage. If she were honest with herself, she did not know which was worse. Mel's thoughts were interrupted by Naomi's lazy murmur.

"C'mon. Time to go catch bad guys."

With a wry smile, Mel rolled over and out of bed. She took one last look at the woman lying in the bed. Light glinted from the small earrings Mel had bought her. Small gold Apache helicopters. What she used to fly. After briefly wondering what that had been like, Mel began to get ready for work. She spent the next 10 minutes going through her judo warm-up stretches. Feeling more alert, she headed out to the kitchen. She began thinking about the night before, and her smile broadened to a grin at the memory of Mick's face. One day, that kid was going to do something, something she couldn't even help with. She set the kettle to make herself a cup of tea. Then, set the coffee maker hissing for Naomi. She would not be up for another hour, but at least the coffee would be better. Mel's thoughts were interrupted by the melodious carolling of the Magpies outside. Smiling, she returned to the fridge and pulled out a packet of dog sausage. Cutting off a small helping, she took it outside. As she stepped through the back door, she greeted the small family of large black and white birds perched around the back patio. Heads cocked, they erupted into another chorus.

"Good morning, maggies. Hello Frank, Matilda. Junior, you've grown again."

They hopped down and gathered at her feet as she crouched. She handed a small piece to each of them. She never had pets, and for some reason, the idea of owning an animal in a confined house felt wrong. However, she was happy to spend time with these beautiful birds. They trusted her, and that trust meant something. Dogs and cats would cosy up to anyone who fed them. Wild animals, on the other hand, needed time and patience to cultivate trust. They came and took the food from her fingers. She often wanted to grab one, to feel those silk feathers. But if she did, Mel knew that would end the trust. Instead, she contented herself with watching, feeding and listening. When they were done, they warbled what Mel called their thank-you song before flying to a nearby gum. Mel waved at them as she turned away.

"You're very welcome," Mel smiled as she headed inside to make herself an omelette.

Forty minutes later, Mel was stepping out of her house. She walked over to her E-bike, perched against the wall. Mounting it, she began her morning ritual of riding to work, mentally assuming the role of Senior Constable Hobson.

Mick peeked out of his bedroom door, head tilted slightly. The house was quiet. He nodded to himself, relieved. His mother was working an early shift. He suddenly frowned. Now he thought about it, he could not remember the last day she had taken off. He felt a slight twist in his gut as he realised she had been working while he had been lounging around on the weekends. She kept talking about the hospital being short-staffed. The pandemic had resulted in many staff being redeployed to other roles, that was, if they were not having to isolate because of testing positive. According to the news, this has led to a nationwide nursing shortage. The remaining nurses were beginning to burn out, trying to fill the gaps that had been left. His jaw clenched. Perhaps he could do more to help. Resolving to ask her about this tonight, he headed to the kitchen to make breakfast. His nose wrinkled as he walked into the kitchen. What was that? Irish Cream? He had come home to find Tilda slumped over the kitchen table, Midnight Oil's *Blue-Sky Mining* playing in a perpetual loop on the CD player. Fearing another argument, Mick had left her there and crept to bed. He felt another pang of guilt about his earlier relief about his mother's absence. *Blue-Sky mining?* She was still hurting about Jerry. He shook himself, knuckling his eye.

"Damn, allergies," he told himself. This was not the way Mick liked to start his day. As he pulled the wheat biscuits out of the cupboard, Mick considered what he might do to get help for Tilda. He dumped five into a bowl, sloshed milk over them and sat at the table, pulling his phone out. Absently crunching his breakfast, he scrolled through possible mental health support services in Emerald. The problem was, Mick thought as he took a swig of his coffee. Emerald was small. Anyone he approached for help might feel inclined to report his mother as unsafe to work. That would not help at all. His brow furrowed. Is that why his mother drank? She was afraid to get help. Worse. She could not afford to get help.

"Fuck," he said to the empty kitchen.

Breakfast finished, Mick stood, gathered his dishes, and added his bowl and cup to the liquor glass, cup, and bowl already in the sink. He turned to head off. Stopped. He turned to study the sink, his focus resting on the glass. He might be unable to help her with all her problems, but perhaps he could start with something small. Glancing at the clock, he nodded. He started at eight. He had time. Mick went over to the sink. He fumbled with the plug and turned on the hot tap. As the sink began to fill, he squirted in a generous amount of concentrated washing-up liquid. He grinned as the head of soap suds began to grow. His phone beeped. By now, the sink was full, and suds had started to flow over the draining board. Ignoring the phone, he cleaned the dishes, reaching through elbow-deep suds to the quarter-filled sink. As he worked, he thought about the night before. He felt his heartbeat in his throat as he thought about Leanne, her cool hands fumbling with his belt, sliding over his stomach, down to his... However, as he wiped down the sideboards, he was surprised to realise he had not been disappointed when Hobson had knocked on the window. Indignant. Yes. Angry. Yes. But he was also relieved. He was not that kind of bloke. He knew Jack would not get it, but Mick wanted his first time to be...special. He knew that blokes were not meant to be like that, but his Dad had once said that you only get one shot at the first time. Make it special. The back of *the Mutant* under a railway bridge was not special. A beach. Up north. A sunset. *That* was special. Stepping back, Mick looked at the washing up on the draining board. Clean and covered in suds. Nodding satisfied, he headed out. He was stepping out into the cool morning. *The Mutant* was where he had left her, covered by a sheen of dew. Mick jumped into the driver's seat, and as he twisted the key and the engine turned, he remembered he had a message waiting. The engine juddered to life. He left *the Mutant* in neutral and pulled out his phone. The group link app icon had a little red 1 in the corner. He was about to flick open the app when he saw the time. It was nearly 0735.

"Shit!"

Shoving his phone into his pocket, he dropped the car into gear and reversed into the street.

Mick made it just in time. Grinning, he rushed into the office, tapping the time clock, which beeped reassuringly with a minute to spare. He walked over to the computer in the corner, turning it on as he sat down. When it had booted up, he tapped his card on the keyboard and logged in. Jack sauntered in as Mick read the emailed instructions from their boss.

"Mornin'," Jack sang as he tapped on the time clock. "I had a grrreat night last night. How'd you fare, bro?"

"Hobson broke us up. Took Leanne home as things were getting interesting," Said Mick with a blush. He did not think he would mention his relief at the interruption.

"Yeah. I saw...briefly. Tough break. What's Hobson's problem? She always seems to be where you are. I wouldn't mind, but this could cause me problems."

Mick shrugged.

"How'd the twin's Dad react to them being dropped off separately?"

"That's the weird thing. Hobson just dropped Leanne off at the front. Didn't wake her folks. No charges. Parents don't know."

"True? Why?"

Jack shrugged.

"I'm just glad *I'm* not in the shit again. Perhaps she likes men after all...but likes 'em young. If she ever cuffs you, I'd watch out."

Mick glared at Jack.

"What? I can't think why else she'd let it slide." Jack jumped back to avoid Mick's kick before continuing, "Well, *I* had a great time if you get my meaning," he made a see-sawing motion with his hand.

Ignoring him, Mick stared at the wall behind Jack's head. Jack had a point. It didn't make sense. Hobson always seemed ready to book him, yet when she got the chance, she never did. There was something she had said yesterday; what was it? Jack interrupted his thoughts.

"Ready for work?"

Mick looked at him, a slight frown creasing his forehead. "You sound keen? Feelin' alright?"

"What can I say? A night like last night makes me..."

Shaking his head, Mick turned and pretended to be busy with emails.

"What? What'd I say? Not even a booyah? I need a booyah. Ah. You're in a mood. I see this now. I'll fill you in later. Give you a blow-by-blow rundown if you get my drift."

Mick ignored that one, too. Jack shrugged.

"OK. Okay. What's the plan? You want the mower or the rake?"

"You choose," Mick murmured, absently clicking the mouse.

A sly grin crept across Jack's face as he walked over to the key rack and took the keys to the ride-on mower. He turned and headed out of the door. Despite himself, Mick grinned. He could not be mad at his mate for long. He sat in the chair, gazing at the monitor. The sound of the ride-on mower cut across the silence.

"Crap."

Suddenly, he remembered Jack was banned from driving ride-on anything. The chair toppled backwards as Mick rushed out of the office. His phone suddenly vibrated with a reminder. Remembering his message, Mick pulled out his phone and flicked open the Grouplink app. Not intending to read the message, he stopped short. He read the message from Con. He reread it, his brow furrowing.

Good morning, Mick. I wanted to let you

know I am cancelling my Grouplink

account tomorrow arvo. I have a face

call from my son at 1100, then I'll be cancelling.

I wanted to say thank you for being there

these past two years. You are a good lad.

Please keep safe. Goodbye. Con.

He read it a few times before the meaning sank in, dammit, now Con was leaving him. Why did people keep letting him down? Kicking himself for not reading it earlier, Mick replied.

What? No man, you're the only life on this platform.

The Mutant *still has a lot of work to do.*

Is everything okay? Did I offend you?

"Yeeeeehaaaa!"

Mick leapt out of the way as Jack roared past him on the mower. He looked back at the message, pressed send, and waited. Not receiving a reply, he headed to the tool shed. At least the bunkers made sense.

29/07/2020.

1130.

Emerald Milk Bar.

Mick sat on *the Mutant's* bonnet outside the milk bar near the golf club, wolfing down a meat pie and a banana. He pulled out his phone and checked his message thread with Con for the third time since he sat down.

Con?

Con?

Con? Are you there?

He had time to think as he raked the sand traps. Mick always found the mindful, regular motion soothing. His anger at Con was misplaced. Rereading the message, he began to feel that Con was in trouble. He thought about the messages Con had sent over the last twenty-four hours. They seemed sad. Down. It was odd, but although he had never met Con, Mick felt close to him. He had guided him through his 4x4 hobby, true. But Con had also, at times, helped him with life. Mick had even mapped out a road trip to show Con the finished *Mutant.* By the time it was lunch, Mick had realised that he regarded Con almost paternally. Had Con sensed that? Had it worried him? Munching absently, Mick thought about the messages. Down mood. He's selling his stuff off and cutting ties. Saying goodbye.

"No," Mick murmured weakly, suddenly feeling sick. Stuffing the last of his banana in his mouth, he closed the Grouplink app and flicked open a search app. His hands were shaking. He looked up mental health services for the second time that day, but this time in Victoria. He looked up Frankston Region

Mental Health Services and pressed their number. The phone rang twice. He waited a moment as he listened to the obligatory message about emergencies and to call 000. Then a man's voice came through his phone.

"Frankston Region Mental Health Triage, this is John. How can I help?"

Suddenly, Mick was stuck for words, unsure what to say.

"Hello," Prompted John, his voice softening. "What's happening?"

Mick cleared his throat.

"Ah, yeah, look, I'm not sure what to do. I think a friend wants to kill himself."

"What makes you say that?"

The response was practised, but now the voice had a tinge of urgency.

"Well...We're friends on Grouplink. Lately, his messages have been sounding...down."

Mick suddenly felt ridiculous.

"How do you mean down?"

"He's normally upbeat, happy. Lately, though, his messages have seemed...down. His last message read something like: *'I'm cancelling my Grouplink tomorrow after I speak to my son at 11:00.'* Then he thanked me for being here for the last two years. And he has been giving stuff away. Well, selling it. Good stuff. Real cheap."

Mick's mind raced as he fit it all together. Why was all this coming to him now?

"Ok. How was he the last time you saw him?"

"I've never seen him. He's too far away."

There was a noticeable pause.

"Cool. Where are you calling from, mate?"

"Queensland."

Mick had a sense this was not going well.

Another pause. This one is longer.

"OK. Here's what I'll do. I'll call the police and get them to do a welfare check on him. How does that sound?"

Mick nodded. Relieved. John sounded kind, if not convinced.

"Cheers. Can you call and let me know how he is?"

"Sure thing, on the number you are calling from now?"

"Yeah."

"What is his name and address?"

Mick gazed for a moment. Stumped. Why had he not anticipated this obvious question? Suddenly, he remembered the box the lights arrived in.

"Gimmie a tick. I got it here somewhere."

Jumping down from the bonnet, he moved to the back door and yanked it open. He rummaged amongst the rubbish under the passenger's seat and pulled out what was left of the packaging the lights had arrived in. He found Con's address on the sender's portion of the package, squinting as he read Con's cursive script.

"Here it is. Ready?"

"Shoot."

"26 Lonicera Street. Frankston North."

"The Pines," Observed John.

"That significant?" asked Mick, unsure what "the Pines" meant.

"Not really. I'll be in touch. Bye."

The phone clicked off. Sliding his phone into his thigh pocket, Mick gazed at the torn brown paper in his hand, thinking about the conversation. What was a welfare check? What did *that* mean? Police. Had he gotten Con in trouble? Had he misread the message? He glanced at his phone and saw the time. Lunch was over. He tossed the paper packaging into the back of *the Mutant* and slammed the door. He climbed into the cab, leaned down, and started the engine. Pulling his phone back out, he dialled Jack's number, and on the third ring, Jack answered.

"Sup?"

"What're you up to at the mo?"

"Watching some lady golfers practising their swing. Why?"

Mick grinned.

"Can you meet me at the shed? I got somethin' I want to show you?"

"What?"

"It's a bit hard. I'll show you in the shed."

"A bit har…Is this something that's going to change our relationship? I'm not totally against the idea, but there are rules 'bout that in the workplace," said Jack.

"Just get to the damn shed."

Wheels spinning, Mick moved *the Mutant* onto the road and headed back to the golf club.

Half an hour later, Mick looked at Jack, who, perched on a barrel of weed killer, was scrolling down the chat thread.

"I see what you mean. It does seem…final," Jack said, uncharacteristically serious.

"It's a worry. I mean, after Dad…left, Con helped me. You know, build *the Mutant*. Helped me source parts. As soon as I had her on the road, I was going to do that road trip to Frankston. I've got the route notes in the glove box. Then the virus hits and fucks that up. You need permits to go through New South and to get into Victoria. They reckon it can take weeks to get them, even in an emergency, if they say yeah. The Victorians are knocking back families. I'm not family. They won't let me in. But I can't lose another…" Mick bit the last word off. He was going to say, Father. Instead, he finished with, "Not like this."

Jack cleared his throat awkwardly. Mick's father was always a shaky subject.

"Have the peeps in Frankston called you back?"

"No."

They sat in silence for several minutes. Each was lost in his thoughts. Jack spoke first.

"Perhaps we should just go? You know. Road trip."

"Us? Go? Are you nuts? Go to Victoria? With restrictions and work? Things with Mum aren't great. I can't just up and leave. And if you get caught, the magistrate'd lock you up, and that's it between you and Jo. Her Dad'd end it."

Jack raised his hands.

"It was just a thought. Your call, of course. I heard on the radio earlier that mental health services nationwide are swamped. They can't give the time they need to people."

"True?"

Jack nodded.

"Plus...be a good test run for *the Mutant*."

Mick considered and then shook his head.

"Yeah, nah. We've got just under twenty-four hours, give or take. That's almost too late, given it'd take twenty-two hours straight driving to get there. Let's wait for the mental health people to get back to us."

"Sure," Jack dropped from the barrel. "Well, gotta bounce. Them lawns won't mow themselves. Keep me posted."

Mick nodded as he watched Jack head out. Pulling out his phone, he flicked open the Grouplink app. He wrote;

Con? You there?

He sat gazing out of the window, considering. A road trip? He had a route planned. The police could not patrol the whole border. He brought himself back to look at the lush green surrounds of the gold club. Most of the time, he found the environment relaxing. Today, he found it frustrating. Constricting. Static. Giving his head a shake to clear it, he decided. He'd wait for Frankston to call. He stood and headed back into the sunshine.

Mick pulled up next to another sand trap, looking at it critically. Turning off the buggy, he climbed out and moved closer, kneeling. The surface had been ruffled, with a few dips and a line of footprints, but it was not unsightly. This one could wait. Nodding, he stood and climbed back into the buggy. Pulling out his phone, he checked for messages and missed calls. He still had not heard from Frankston. Mick unlocked the phone again and accessed the call log. He pressed the number for Frankston Mental Health. This time, the wait was longer. Eventually, a female answered the phone.

"Good afternoon. Mental health services. You are speaking to Deepam; how may I help you?"

The different voice surprised Mick. He should not have been, now he thought about it. It was unlikely that there would be only one person staffing a help desk.

"Er, hi, Deepam. Could I speak to John, please?"

"John is on his break at the moment. What is this about?"

Mick paused a moment and then, with a shrug, plunged on.

"Ah, yeah. Um. I called earlier. I'm ringing from Queensland. It was about a man named Con. Lives on the Pines? I think that's what John said."

"Ah, yes. That was handed over. The police have done a welfare check. John was going to call you when he got a moment. The police found the gentleman to be as well as can be expected."

"Ok. So he's alright?"

There was a pause.

"Yes."

Mick frowned. He had the sense she was not telling him everything.

"Is there anything else?"

"Unfortunately, I cannot go into details due to confidentiality, but yes, he is at home and settled."

Mick frowned. How could he ask the questions he wanted so they would answer?

"So, he's okay. I mean, it sounded like he wanted to…to die."

There was another pause as the lady on the other end chose her words.

"As okay as can be expected."

"What does that mean? Is he okay or not? It's a simple question for fff…" Mick drew a deep breath. "Do we know why he seems down?"

"I'm sorry, sir, but I cannot discuss the details unless you are a family member. Have you tried contacting him yourself?"

"Yeah. He didn't reply."

"Well. Keep trying; I'm sure he will reply. Now, is there anything else I can do for you?"

Mick sighed, but through his clenched jaw, it came out as more of a whistle.

"No. Thanks," He cut the call.

Mick stood for a moment, thinking. What was going on with Con? Looking back at his phone. He typed.

Hi Con. I'm a bit worried about you. Can you message me when you get this?

Mick was sliding his phone back into his pocket when it beeped. He whipped it out.

Micky boy. Stop worrying about me.

I am fine. Thank you for your concern. Now get back to work.

Mick stared at the message for several minutes.

"Perhaps we should go." Jack had said. The afternoon heated up as he shifted his gaze to the sand trap. He began to imagine he could see each grain individually. The sound of flies, birds. The occasional yell of "Fore!" faded as he thought. He could feel sweat dripping down his face, soaking into his collar. The whole time, Jack's voice floated around his head.

"Perhaps we should go."

Con was troubled, Mick was certain. He had not replied to the last messages. Something was wrong with the man, and by eleven tomorrow morning, he would do something terrible. Saying goodbyes. Mick's head snapped up. Pulling out his phone again, he called Jack. He began speaking before Jack had finished his: "Sup."

"Hey, mate. I think tomorrow at eleven, Con is going to say goodbye to his son. I think tomorrow midday he's going to...kill himself," He struggled to get the last bit out. There was a moment of silence before Jack spoke, his tone cautious.

"Man, you sure?"

Mick nodded as he continued, "I'm heading off on that road trip to Frankston. If I leave now and drive through the night, I should get there in time. I need you to cover for me."

"Hey? Wait? What? Dude, wait up; I'll come," Jack said excitedly.

"Nah, you need to stay here. This is something I need to do. Perhaps if I can stop him...look, I need to do this. On my own."

"No way," Jack protested. "This is the most badass thing you've ever done. You don't do badass. I'm the badass king. You'll need me."

"OK. If you want to help, I need you to stay here. Cover for me. I'll tell Mum we're camping this weekend. I need you to distract Hobson and keep her thinking I'm in town. That sorta thing."

"What? Like driving around with a standee in the car. Attach it to strings-"

"This is serious, man."

"Fuck, you think I don't know? You can't drive all that way on your own. What happens if you crash? How's that going to help? You need a second driver. If not me, then someone else."

"No! Too risky. If I get caught, I don't want to be responsible for getting others in the shit."

"But-"

"If you come, and we get caught, what happens?"

There was another longer pause, and then Jack's voice came in. Thick. Husky.

"Fuck, I wish I was not such a fuckin dick. If I'd not-"

Mick felt a twist in his gut. He had not intended his friend to resent himself.

"Jack. Man, you are the best mate a bloke could want. Don't look like that, I mean it," because he could picture Jack's face. "But I need someone I can trust here. Keeping an eye on Mum, watching Hobson. When I get back, I'll have it out with her. But this... man... this is something I need to do. If I can stop Con, maybe it'll go away to fixing...stuff,"

Jack coughed, clearing his throat.

"Dude, he's gone. He's not coming back. You know that."

"I know. But perhaps I can save some pain somewhere else. I mean, Con has a family. A wife. I *need* to try. This is *my* fight."

Jack paused again. This time longer. Mick began to wonder if the call had dropped. He looked at his phone. It was connected.

"Jack?"

"Ok. Keep an eye on your Mum."

"Please."

"Watch the Terminatrix."

Mick nodded.

"It won't be easy. It's you she has a crush on. You're the one she keeps following."

Jack sounded normal again.

"Fuck you. Just do it, will you?"

"OK. But you'll owe me. I've been stuck in this town like you for months. I'm going batshit crazy too."

"I'll just take it from the thousands of favours you owe me."

"Oh, and Mick?"

"Yeah?"

"In all seriousness, leaving me alone with your mother, don't be surprised if she can't keep her hands off me."

Mick cut the call. He headed back to the maintenance shed.

30/07/2020.

1400.

Sato Service Station.

Mick pulled into the Sato service station and parked in the bay next to the door. As he climbed out, he looked around. He could see no sign of Akina in the forecourt. After filling his tank to the brim, he walked into the shop and was relieved to see it was Akina's grandfather, Sato Senior, behind the counter. The elderly Japanese looked up as the bell above the door tinkled. His eyes narrowed above the mask, below which wisps of a white beard sprang out. He made a stop gesture and pointed to the "no mask, no service" sign. Irritably, feeling the seconds tick away, Mick returned to *the Mutant* and pulled a mask from a stash under the sunshade. As he turned back, he looped the elastic strings around his ears. Akina blocked his way. She had a backpack over her shoulder. Her eyes blazed. Mick stumbled back to avoid ploughing into her.

"Where'd you spring from?"

He could not keep the surprise from his voice.

"You filled up yesterday."

Gritting his teeth, Mick nodded.

"Yeah. I'm going bush with Jack tonight. We need munchies."

Her eyebrow arched.

"Really. Bush. With Jack."

Mick had a sense of déjà vu.

"Yeah."

The silence was awkward. She glared at him, and not for the first time in the last twenty-four hours, Mick felt his heart sink. It was the silent game. Again.

"You do know Jack has my phone number, right?"

Mick closed his eyes. Dammit Jack.

"For fu...Look, Akina, Jack had no right dragging you into this-"

"He has every right. He's your best mate. I'm your...mate. He's worried about you. So am I. A twenty-four-hour road trip. That's a day. That's too much driving. You'll crash and die. Then we will never-"

"It's not like I'd be missed."

Akina's eyes flared wider.

"You selfish sonofabitch. Your Mum. Jack. Me. We all love you, and if you pulled your head out of your ass long enough, you'd realise how much."

Her words were a slap. He shook his head, trying to clear it.

"Wait. What? You-"

"Just go fucktard. I don't care anymore."

Akina stalked off towards the workshop.

"Akina. Wait."

He moved to follow, then looked at the time. He had to get moving. He only had until eleven tomorrow, and Hobson would be looking for him in two hours. He did not want to lose Con. Everyone in Emerald he could reconcile with when he got back, but if Con died... Shaking his head, Mick headed back into the convenience shop.

"Hello. How are you?" sang out Sato Senior, his English heavy with his Japanese accent.

"Great, thanks, Mr Sato, Sir. You?"

"Good. What can I do for you?"

"The fuel and some supplies. Me and Jack are heading out camping today," said Mick as he walked around pulling items off the shelves.

"Ah. Boys will be boys. But why come here? Supermarket cheaper. We rip you off."

"Well, I don't want word getting out I am buying a lot of food. Police might think I am having a party or something."

"Ah. Good plan. Your secret safe," Laughed Sato Senior, tapping his nose. He began ringing up the supply of food.

Mick looked around the service station forecourt as he headed back to *the Mutant, munching on a meat pie from the pie warmer.* Akina was nowhere in sight. He was both disappointed and relieved. He considered looking for her. Did she love him? What did she mean by that? Did she mean as a best friend, or...it was what he had wanted. For years. Was that why she was so weird yesterday? The condoms and the date. It made sense. He stopped and looked around again. He *should* look for her. Strike while the iron was hot. But he was already against the clock. He opened the door of *the Mutant* and threw the bags of chips, water, and chocolates into the passenger's foot well. Stuffing the last of his pie in his mouth, he climbed in. Reaching the glove compartment, he pulled the Frankston road trip notes from the glove box. Mick had not looked at them for months, leaving them there, thinking he could use them when restrictions lifted. He studied the printout of the maps, reading the instructions he had written on them. Nodding, he tossed them into the passenger seat. He started the motor and pulled slowly away. Taking one last look around for Akina, he turned the wheel and pulled into the street. He took the third exit at the roundabout and headed south along the Gregory Highway.

First, he took it easy, driving on the limit, not wanting to attract attention. He kept an eye on the rear-view mirror, looking out for Hobson. Once he was further along the highway, he was able to put his foot down and make up some time.

His mind ran through the messages left by Con. He had until about eleven o'clock. Midday the next day at the latest, assuming Con did not rush the call. For some reason, Mick doubted he would. What did the man plan? Would it be at home? If not, then where? Why tomorrow? What was the significance of that day? That time? Before long, however, Mick found his mind wandering. This was the first time since his Dad had left that he had been south on the Gregory. It stirred fond and painful memories of fishing trips off the shores of Lake Maraboon and nights camping under the stars. He smiled tightly as he passed the turn-off to the Fairbairn State Forest, where he and his Dad used to camp.

He remembered when he was twelve. He and his Dad had pulled off the dirt track near a small, clear patch near the lake. They had climbed out of the four-wheel drive and began pulling gear off racks on the back. They set up their swags, built a fire and then went fishing for their tea. After the exertion, his Dad would always need a little time to catch his breath. Mick's jaw clenched, remembering he would make fun of the mega-fit desk cop, inviting him to join him at the gym. His father would laugh and offer a wrestling match, which, as a trained cop, he would always win. The humour was good when they were camping. Mick's Dad was the self-proclaimed king of the Dad joke. Mick could not remember specific conversations or specific jokes. Just the groans and laughter. Tips on fishing. The art of packing an overnight pack.

"Always have emergency undies on your rig."

His Dad used to say. There had been times his mother had come, too. But the days when it was just him and his Dad had been the most special. Before Jerry had left. Gritting his teeth angrily, Mick flicked on the CD player and lost himself to ACDC's Razor's Edge Album. He slowed down again as he passed through Springsure; looking at his trip notes, the car wobbled slightly as he took a right branch onto the road which headed out of town.

Jack pulled his Patrol out of the car park and headed towards his home. He considered calling Mick to see how he was doing. The yelp of a siren behind him caused him to look in the rear-view mirror, though he knew who it would be. He groaned. It *was* Hobson. The lights of her Land Cruiser flashed. She wanted him to pull over. He did so. It took a few moments for Hobson to approach the driver's side window. Jack eyed her athletic form appreciatively as she moved up the side of his rig. He wondered if the rumours about Hobson not liking men were true. In a town like Emerald, rumours tended to fly, and although his generation did not care, the older inhabitants could be a little old-fashioned. He wound down the window.

"Fine afternoon, constable, 'sup?"

"Can you turn your engine off, please, Jack?"

Straight to business. No small talk. Jack hated that. Without small talk, he could not charm his way out of trouble. His mind raced, trying to remember what speed he had been going. He leaned down and turned off the engine.

"What's this about?"

"Leaving work a bit early, aren't you?"

"Yeah, well, you know. Weekend and all. It's not illegal...is it? I lose track of what we can and can't do these days."

Now, he considered it, given that he was on a government scholarship, there might be attendance ramifications with his course.

"Not like Mick to leave early."

Jack stared. Not knowing what she knew, Jack was not sure what to say. It was not a question, so Jack stayed silent. Hobson continued.

"Seems you had a good night last night. It could be quite expensive, though. You know, if I were to charge you. And you are on a bond, too. Could cost you more than a fine."

Jack nodded, again opting for silence.

"Where's O'Hare?"

The question took Jack by surprise.

"Mick?"

Hobson nodded.

"Yeah. Just left him at work."

"True?"

"Hundred per cent."

"It's just that I happened to pass the club. I saw you leave. I waited a few minutes. I didn't see O'Hare leave. I took a drive through the carpark. His truck's not there either. He's not on another date? Making up for last night?"

She looked for him. In the carpark? Not for the first time, Jack was fascinated by Hobson's obsession with Mick.

"Don't know what to say. I last saw him at the club. You must've missed him."

Hobson's radio crackled, and she turned away to speak into it briefly. Jack could not make out the whole conversation clearly, and he felt uneasy. After a couple of moments, she turned back. He shifted uneasily in his seat as she looked at him for several moments. Her face under the mask and sunglasses was unreadable. Suddenly, she waved Jack on.

"Move on. Straight home now. Don't let me see you out tonight."

"Sure thing, constable. And you stay safe, ma'am."

Starting the motor, Jack pulled away. He glanced into his rearview and saw Hobson as she climbed into her car and pulled into the traffic, lights blazing. He flicked the control, which linked his car stereo to his phone.

"Call TrickyMicky."

After a few moments, the phone rang. Mick answered.

"What's up, Jack?"

"Just had a run-in with the Terminatrix. She's on to you, dude."

"Already? You tell *her* about the road trip," Said Mick.

"Why would I?"

"You told Akina."

Jack winced.

"OH, that. She with you?"

"Of course not."

"Look, dude, I hate the thought of you on that drive alone. You should have someone to share the driving with. You're right, jail for me if we were caught, but I thought, given how you felt for her-"

"That's why she can't come. Her Dad'll kill me if I take her. Look, man, she's too important to me. I won't risk losing whatever friendship I can get."

"OK. Chill out. Look, just keep a lookout. I think Hobson's on the prowl. She doesn't know anything concrete, but there are ways to track people through phones."

"Yeah, well, I'll have to cross that one when the time comes." Mick sounded irritated.

"Catchya, Bro."

Mick cut the call. Jack shook his head and looked around. He was in such deep thought that he did not even realise where he had been driving until he pulled up the drive to his home.

30/07/2020.

1730.

Emerald.

She woke herself up with her snore. Tilda jerked awake from an exhausted snooze. She looked around the room self-consciously. Then she felt ridiculous for feeling self-conscious about snoring. Her mouth was dry, and her tongue felt like rough rubber. It was getting more challenging these days. She had worked overtime again at the COVID clinic and came straight home as required. She looked at her half-finished glass of wine and reached for it. Her hand stopped midway. She cocked her head, listening for Mick's rock music.

"Mick?" she called out.

No answer.

"MICHAEL!"

She was alone in the house.

When she got home after her double shift, Tilda kicked off her shoes, slumped into her chair, and switched on the television. The news. She poured herself a glass of wine from the half-finished bottle on the table and fell asleep.

She frowned as she looked at the clock on the wall. It was five thirty-five. Where was Mick? She checked her phone. No messages. No missed calls

Usually, he would have called to check if she needed groceries for dinner. He would then ask her to put the kettle on. Tossing the phone on the table, she stood. Moving stiffly at first, Tilda went to Mick's room. She tapped on the door. When there was no answer, she pushed open Mick's door and looked in. The Floor was littered with dirty underwear, T-shirts and jeans. The mixture of sweat and deodorant assaulted her nose as she studiously ignored the stiffened tissues on the floor next to the bed. His four-wheel drive magazines were scattered around the floor, but Mick was not sprawled on the bed reading one. Frowning, she closed the door and walked back through to the kitchen. Tilda put the jug on. She walked back to the front room to look out the window. Her car was alone in the driveway. Tilda returned to the front room, picked up her phone and tried to dial Mick's number. The phone went immediately to voicemail. That was odd. But not the first odd thing for the day. Mick had washed up. She looked at the glass on the table. It was the one Mick had washed. She had been surprised to find it clean, though not rinsed. Her wine tasted of washing-up liquid.

Picking up her phone, Tilda tried calling again. After a few moments, she got the 'phone is non-contactable' message. So she sent him a message;

Where r u?

Looking out the window, she muttered, "What are you up to now, you idiot?"

Mick looked at the clock on the dashboard of his car. He was making good time. He had been averaging just over 100 km, which was not bad given that he had slowed to 80 km for unsealed stretches of road. He looked ahead and saw the sign welcoming people to Tambo. He stretched, his jaw cracking as he yawned. *The Mutant* swerved as he stretched, snapping back his focus.

"Perhaps you should let me drive for a bit."

With a yell, Mick swerved off the road, skidding to a halt in a cloud of red dust. The truck lurched as the engine stalled. Mick sat gripping the wheel, breathing heavily as Akina climbed from the back seat. Mick glared at the girl now in the passenger seat.

"What the fuck Akina! Are you trying to get us killed?" he yelled.

For the first time in his life, he was not happy to see her.

"What? Perhaps I should have jumped up and yelled surprise?"

"No. I mean…"

Mick's mouth worked, but no other words came out. He did not know what to say. So, he said nothing. He started the engine and pulled back onto the road, driving through the settling dust. Akina grinned at him. "Yeah. I couldn't stay there for much longer. It's bumpy as."

Akina shrank a little under Mick's glare.

"Why are you even here?" his voice was cold.

"I told you. Jack called and told me what was going on. I thought you needed company."

"I need people to stop telling me what's best for me. What I need is for people to back the hell off. Give me a break, and let me do my thing. Your Dad's going to be furious about…"

Mick's voice tailed off as he remembered the call with Jack, on speaker.

"Look, Mick, like I said, we care about you."

"Really?"

"Really. If you weren't so self-absorbed, you'd see it."

"Me? Self-absorbed? Who invited herself on a road trip? Who hid in the back of a car? Eh? Did it occur to you I wanted to be by myself for a bit?"

"Kinda proves my point."

"Look, if I was selfish, I'd invited everyone along. Said fuck it, they can cop the $1400 fine, the six months in jail. Jack can lose his scholarship and freedom. They can have a criminal record. No, I was goin' to wear that one on my own. If I get caught, the way things stand, it'll be my first offence. I'd be okay. If Jack got caught, he'd end up in the slammer 'cause of his recog. Lose his job. If you get caught, you'll have a record. That means going to Japan would be difficult, you know, when the world opens back up. PLUS, there's nothin' selfish about needing time alone."

"True. But sneaking away? Not telling anyone?" said Akina, hurriedly moving the conversation on from her.

Mick looked at her.

"I'm not sneaking."

"Really? Have you told your mom you've gone?"

This last point hit him like a hammer. His mother. He had not told his mother. He had not even considered her. He had initially not told her because she would have tried to stop him. Would probably have called Hobson. She would be worried about her precious position and what having him break the law would look like for her. But then guilt welled up. The last thing he wanted was for her to think he was leaving her. Running away. Why had he not thought about her? Perhaps he was selfish. In some ways, at least. He looked at the clock. It was well past the time he would have been home. But what should he say to her? What should he do about Akina?

"Just shut up a minute."

Was all he could think of saying as he pulled back onto the highway.

He was still thinking of his mother when his phone buzzed twenty minutes later. He looked at his phone, mounted in its bracket on the dashboard. He was back at one bar reception in a couple of hours for the first time. It was missed call notifications and messages from his mother and Jack. They entered Tambo and saw a service station on the side of the road. Mick pulled onto the forecourt and switched off the motor. They sat. The only sound was the ticking of the cooling engine. As Mick opened the door, Akina reached for the handle. He looked across at her.

"Just stay in the car. I need to think," He snapped as he stepped out of the rig.

"Mick," Called Akina.

He ignored her, slamming the door and causing the vehicle to rock gently.

"Mick!" Her voice whipped through the open window. He stopped looking at her as she pointed to her face.

"Mask?"

Closing his eyes for a moment, Mick stalked back to the car. He snatched his mask from the dashboard and walked around to the bowser. It was one of the old-school types with rotating dials. He did not *need* to fill up, but it gave him the time to think. How dare Akina? This was *his* problem. She thought she could just ...jump in. Interfere? He was trying to keep her out of trouble, and she just invited herself along. The pump ticked to a stop. He looked at the number and went in.

"How's it goin'?" asked the woman behind the desk. Her name tag read, 'Hi, I'm Jessica.' She was in her thirties. She could have been a customer in her blue flannel shirt and jeans.

"Great, thanks, pump one, " Mick said as he walked over to the fridge and pulled out two colas.

"I see that. It's not like it's rush hour."

"Right."

"Road trip to the sand banks?"

"Something like that. Look, my friend's kinda unwell, but. Is there a bus to Emerald?" He asked, pulling his wallet out of his back pocket and extracting his bank card. Jessica's eyebrows arched.

"Emerald? A bit out of your LGA, aren't you?"

"Yeah, well...you won't dob us in, will you?"

"Depends. What exactly do you mean when you say unwell?" asked Jessica suspiciously.

Mick suddenly recognised the hole in his ruse. He kicked himself. Thinking quickly, he said, "Anxious. She was coming with me to rebel against her old man. Changed her mind. The bus?"

Jessica's eyes narrowed as she rang up the purchase. She paused for a moment, remembering happier times. Then, suddenly, she focused back on Mick, blushing slightly as she gestured to the EFTPOS. Then she brightened up.

"I won't dob you in. I was young once. That'll be 55 bucks, please."

Very happy times, mused Mick, tapping his card. Jessica continued.

"Hard days for kids in love. I think the bus leaves tomorrow morning. About 0530. If you'd like, you can camp down the road. There's a small forest. You can drop 'er off at the stop first thing,"

"Yeah. I might do that. Thanks," smiled Mick. There was the swag rolled up on the rack of *the Mutant.* He could leave Akina and carry on.

"Have a great trip. I hope you sort out your woes," called Jessica as Mick walked away.

"Cheers," He called back, giving an absent-minded wave as the door closed behind him.

"No," was Akina's simple response when he told her his plan. She sat on *the Mutant's* bonnet, her arms resting casually on her lap, gripping her cola in her hand. She took the occasional swig as they spoke.

"But..."

"NO! I'm coming with you. You need help, company, and someone to share the driving. You can't survive on energy drinks and junk food alone."

Mick looked at her helplessly.

"But..."

She arched an eyebrow. He sighed. He could see Jessica watching them from the window. He suddenly became very conscious that they were where they should not be. He held his hands up.

"Ok."

Akina smiled triumphantly as she hopped down and moved to the driver's seat.

"You have a rest. I'll drive for a bit."

Mick opened his mouth to argue, then thought better of it. What was the point? Unless he was prepared to tie her up and throw her on the bus, and he was sure there was a law against that. He hesitated a moment longer before throwing the keys at her. Which she promptly caught and threw back. He caught them deftly.

"I've still got the ones you gave me when I was helping you with the dual battery set-up," she grinned as she adjusted the mirror.

Shaking his head, he moved to the passenger side.

"Ready." She snapped as he climbed in.

He nodded as she started the motor and moved the gear shift into first. She pressed the accelerator, moving up the gears as she pulled onto the highway.

Hobson looked at the concerned man standing before her.

"She's gone missing. She's late for tea. She's never late for tea. And she's not answering her phone."

Hobson looked at Mr Sato Junior, uncertain how to take this report. Kids did not go missing in Emerald. They ran away, sure, but then there were notes, messages, and sometimes a history of domestic reports and fights. A lead-up. For a brief moment, she thought back to her youth, then slammed the memory away. The past was the past. She focused on the here and now. Kids did not disappear. But he *was* worried. She had learned to trust her parents with that.

"So, you saw her last...when?"

"Dad saw her with Mick O'Hare just past two. They were talking. He bought lots of snacks. Going camping, he said. With Jack."

Hobson's smooth brow furrowed. O'Hare. She might have guessed. At first, he seemed to vanish, but now Akina seemed to have gone. Coincidence? Not to her mind.

"Past two, you say. Your Dad definitely saw her with Michael O'Hare past two?"

Mr Sato nodded. Hobson made a mental note to go and visit Jack. If he was not with Mick but covering for him, then there was more to this.

"Did she go with Mick, maybe? Run away. Have there been problems at home? Boyfriends? Girlfriends?"

"No. Dad reckons it was only him in the truck when he left. She's a good girl. Focused on her schooling. We've had no big fights. The only boy she hangs with is Mick, and he's a good boy too."

Hobson looked at him with a neutral expression, turning over in her mind what he said. There was something in the wording.

"No *big* fights. So you have been fighting?"

"Well, yes, but not big rows. Just the usual stuff. What uni to go to? Where to go on a gap year? That sort of thing. Nothing bitter. Nothing big."

Hobson suppressed a sigh. How many times in her career had she heard that one? She looked at the shorter man in front of her, thinking about what he said. Arguments about the future? Hobson could not think of anything bigger for a teen, particularly during these times. She realised she could not picture Akina, which meant she had not had to talk to her. Usually, a good thing.

"Look, I'll keep an eye out for her. Ask around. Do you have a recent photo of her you can send me?"

Sato nodded, pulling out his phone.

She was starting to get a bad feeling about this. Mick seemed to have disappeared. Jack was playing games. Now Akina had vanished. Each one of these events by itself was nothing. Not worth worrying about. But these three had one thing in common. Mick. They were up to something. They might not be bad kids. Generally. But throw hormones into the mix, and you end up with all sorts of impulsive behaviours. Not bad behaviours. Just impulsive. The trouble is impulsive fun, which could put them on the wrong side of the law. Affect their future.

"Have you tried the…"

Hobson's voice tailed off as she realised there was nowhere to try because everywhere was shut. Her radio crackled, and Hobson leaned in to listen. Another peeping Tom, the address, caused her to stop. She had been there in the last couple of days to investigate the same complaint. Frowning, she turned her attention back to Mr Sato. She ignored her phone, which was now buzzing in her pocket.

"Look, I have to go. As I say, most of the time, in these cases, kids are just out and lose track of time. Can you let me know when she calls or comes back?" She handed him her card, which had her details on it.

He took it with a nod, looked it carefully over before putting it in his shirt pocket.

"And don't forget the photo," said Hobson with a frown.

Mr Sato nodded, his cheeks wobbling. By the time she stepped out into the cooling evening air, her phone had buzzed again. She looked at the call register. It was Tilda O'Hare. Hobson rolled her eyes as she dialled back.

"Hi, Tilda. Mel here. What's up?"

"Have you seen Michael this evening?"

"No. Why?" suddenly attentive.

"He's not answering his phone. I rang Jack, and he said he and Mick were off camping. Heading to Crystal Creek State Forest."

"You want me to go and bring 'em back?"

"No. Yes. Well…"

"Tilda? What have I missed?"

"It's just that I've just had a ping from the bank. A withdrawal. Michael has just used his card in Tambo."

Hobson looked southwards, forehead creasing.

"Tambo? What'd he be doing in Tambo?"

"I don't know."

The strain in Tilda's voice was palpable.

"Should I lock his card?"

Hobson considered.

"No. It's a handy way to keep track of his whereabouts. Besides, denying him resources to survive will achieve nothing."

"Look, he's a good boy. We both know that. But the way things are at the moment…the way they've been. And he hasn't had a chance to recover from his father…you know. He's not in a good place. Whatever he's up to. This could get him into trouble."

Hobson could hear the tension in Tilda's usually calm voice.

"Leave it with me, Tilda. I need to follow up on a call, but I'll get onto the Tambo thing in a bit," snapped Hobson, ending the call. She stared at her police car for a moment. Tambo? What the actual fuck was that idiot up to now? Perhaps he *had* lost his card. Hobson considered calling Tilda back and telling her to lock the card after all. Somehow, that did not gel for her. She shook her head. Soon, Mick will push his luck to a point where even *she* could not help him. Her phone buzzed again. She looked. It was a picture message. She did not recognise the number. Opening the picture, she saw a young Asian girl in dungarees leaning against the bonnet of *the Mutant*. Akina. She took a moment to zoom in on the girl's face, absorbing it. Then she put the phone away and climbed into her car. Seconds later, the lights on the roof flared, and she raced off to Emerald Flats.

Forty minutes later, Hobson pulled up outside Jack's house. The peeper was long gone before she arrived. She spoke to the complainant, an old high school acquaintance. Sarah Mancini. Sarah was also her boss's sister. Sometimes, the size of this town was inconvenient. Since high school, Sarah had married and divorced, and when the child was with the father, the peeper seemed to visit. Hobson took the details and moved on. Another day, she would have patrolled around, but today she had something else to think about. As she walked up the cracked drive, she considered handing the issue of Mick over to someone who was not personally involved. But then that would mean he would be in trouble if caught up to no good.

"Dick head," she hissed under her breath as she walked up the drive. Hobson noted Jack's Patrol was parked on the neatly trimmed lawn. She laid her hand on the bonnet. It was cool. Hobson headed up the drive. She found Jack's Dad, Jack Senior, working on his HQ Monaro GTS in his garage. A short man, he was a darker, older version of Jack. Sweat glistened on his skin, and with a suspicious glare, he snapped, "What do you want? Whatever it was, you can't pin it on Jack. Jack's been here since five."

Hobson tore her eyes away from the beautiful car.

"I just need a quick word with him. I'm looking for Michael O'Hare."

Jack's eyebrows rose with surprise. Police looking for Mick was a first.

"Micky? What's he supposed to have done? He's a good boy. Kept my Jack out of trouble."

"Can I just speak to Jack, please?"

Jack regarded Hobson for a moment, not aggressively, but not exactly welcoming. He turned his head and bellowed over his shoulder.

"Jack. Get out here."

Hobson flinched slightly at the bellow. After a few moments, Jack came out of the door. His eyes widened at the sight of Hobson before he looked at his father.

"Yeah, da?"

"You seen Mick?"

"Not since this arvy. Why?"

"He seems to have disappeared," Replied Hobson, taking over the conversation. "Now, it seems Akina Sato has also disappeared. When two kids go missing, we need to investigate seriously. When exactly did you last see Mick?"

"I told you this 'arvy. It was after work."

"You're lying."

"Prove it," Interjected Jack Senior.

Hobson's jaw clenched.

"You can't, can you?"

This buoyed the younger man. He grinned.

"Yeah. Prove it."

"Shut it," Snapped Jack Senior and Jack seemed to shrink slightly.

Mel shot an exasperated look at the older man. If it had just been Jack, she would have had the younger man talking by now.

"Look, he was last seen at the Sato Servo, buying food. Lots of it. He said he was going camping with you. Is this true?"

"Mick's talking shit. Jack's not camping. He's helping me with the HQ. Right?"

"This true?" asked Hobson.

Jack nodded vigorously, looking like he wanted to be anywhere but here. Hobson gave them a moment longer. She considered pressing the point about Mick being seen out of work at about 1400, contradicting what Jack said. Then decided against it. She did not want to start a fight over something that would not add to what she already knew.

"Thank you for your time. Please let me know if you recall anything."

Hobson said as she turned towards her Cruiser. A large amount of food. Enough for two on a road trip, perhaps? With the Sato girl? But where? And why? Whatever the answer, the timing is right. Hobson looked at her watch. It was nearly six. If Mick *had last been* seen at 1400 in Emerald, he could have passed through Tambo a short while ago. She had to get to him, but he had a hell of a head start. Leaning against her police cruiser, she pulled out her phone and pressed a number in her contacts.

"Hi Nomi, how are you, beautiful?"

"Hey, gorgeous. I'm fine, but wonderin' what time you'll be home?"

Hobson winced, "I won't be home tonight, but I have a favour to ask. Are you able to fly at night?"

"Sure thing. I can fly anywhere, any when."

"Can you land at Tambo?"

"Come again?"

"You heard right. Tambo. How long will it take?"

There was a rustle of papers as Naomi checked her charts.

"With prep about 90 mins."

"Can you take me?" Hobson asked, biting her lip.

Naomi paused a moment.

"The bird needs to stretch her wings anyway, so why not? I'll get her ready, and we can fly as soon as you get here. What's going on?"

Hobson turned, climbing into the cruiser.

"Great, I'll be at the aerodrome in about fifteen. Something's come up. I'll explain when I get there."

"Another search?"

Hobson blushed.

"No, not another search, though the last one ended well for us, don't you think?"

Hobson ended the call and dialled again, speaking as she climbed into her car.

"What is it, Hobson?" snapped Sergeant Mancini.

"Hey, Sarge. Look, I've come over crook. I need to clock off," she said.

There was a moment of silence. "When you say crook…"

"I don't think it's the virus. It's approaching my time of the month-"

"OK, I don't need to hear anymore," Mancini cut in hurriedly, "Just make sure you do a test and take some fucking paracetamol tomorrow. How'd it go with Sarah?"

Hobson winced. She had hoped this wouldn't come up.

"Same, same, boss. By the time I got there, the perp had fucked off. Look, this is starting to get weird; I wonder if a regular patrol through the Flats might be prudent."

"Agreed. I'll get you to swing past tomorrow and tell her we are doing that."

"Yes, boss."

Mancini's tone seemed to soften.

"You just get yourself well."

"Thank you, boss. I'll call you tomorrow," she cut the call.

"I'm sorry, Ms Hobson, but you are wrong. The flag of England is the Union Jack."

Jimmy Atherton's hand shot up.

"Excuse me, Miss."

Mrs Fortescue paused and, with a long-suffering sigh, said, "Yes, Jimmy."

Jimmy, suddenly unsure about the attention he had attracted, turned bright red. He adjusted his glasses and glanced across at Mel, who smiled encouragingly. His face turned a deeper red before he ploughed on.

"The flag of England, miss. Only it's not the Union Jack. The Union Jack, or the Union Flag as it's known in certain circumstances, is of the United Kingdom...a combination of the flags of Scotland, Ireland and England. The flag of England is the George Cross. So technically, Mel's right."

"I think you will find it is the Union Jack."

Mrs Fortescue was seething. How dare this boy lecture her?

"No, miss. Not the flag of England. The flag of-"

A harsh voice cut across the class, causing a snigger to ripple through the group.

"Ah, shut up, Y fronts. You're not her type. She likes-"

"That's enough," Mrs Fortescue's voice silenced the boy's. She looked at Jimmy. "Young man, I spent twelve months in England back in 1981. Don't you think I would know?"

Jimmy looked abashed.

"I…er…lived there for 10 years. My Mum and Dad're from there."

"Pomm-"

"ENOUGH! If I have to speak to you again, William's, you can keep me company after school."

Mrs Fortescue turned her attention back to Jimmy, ignoring the discreet ruffle of papers as students packed away their books.

"OK. What I shall do is go to the library. I shall go and get the Encyclopedia Britannica. You will read the entry about the flag to the class."

Mrs Fortescue strode out of the room. As the door shut, a barrage of paper pellets flew towards Jimmy, who, with a practised move, held up his binder, deflecting most of them. He and Mel exchanged grins as Mrs Fortescue returned to class.

"It would seem Melanie was not wrong."

That was all she said.

"And Jimmy. I think you owe Jimmy an apology," Mel said mildly.

Mrs Fortescue gave Mel a look of pure venom as she turned around slowly.

"Excuse me?"

"Well, he was 'not wrong', and you were-"

The bell sounded. There was a scraping of chairs and a clatter of books and binders closing as the class emptied.

"Goodbye, everyone," Mrs Fortescue said to the students' backs.

As always, Jimmy and Mel were the last to leave. Looking around the classroom to ensure it was empty, Mrs. Fortescue smiled tightly and spoke.

"Of course. I am sorry I was so impolite."

"Thank you," said Jimmy as Mel burst out.

"So you humiliate him in public but apologise in private. Very brave."

"You may leave now," Mrs Fortescue snapped, glowering over her half-rimmed glasses.

Mel took a breath to argue, her eyes ablaze, when Jimmy spoke over her.

"C'mon, Mel, we should be getting out of here."

Mel looked at Jimmy and then at their geography teacher, who was already busy packing away her papers. With a shrug, Mel grabbed her backpack. They walked out of the classroom together and headed towards the lockers.

"I think you upset her," said Jimmy.

"Meh, what's one more person annoyed with me?"

"I'm not annoyed."

Jimmy had gone bright red again.

"Thanks."

"Have you lost weight?"

Mel blushed slightly. She had lost weight and had toned up with the judo training.

"A little. I'm not trying to. I've just been training."

They stood at the intersection where the corridors crossed.

"Er…I'm this way," said Jimmy, indicating the opposite direction Mel was heading.

"Have a good weekend," Said Mel with a smile.

"I will. I'm getting my new computer this weekend. It's got a 24 GB DDR3 chip, which has a bus clock speed of up to 1066 MHz and consumes nearly 30% less power…"

Jimmy stopped mid-sentence, looking at Mel's slightly amused but affectionate expression.

"I meant any social stuff. Date? That sort of thing."

Jimmy looked hurt for a moment.

"Not after last time. I should have guessed it was a setup when she asked me to wear Y-fronts. I don't think I'll live that one down."

"Yeah, well, Sarah is a bitch," growled Mel, wishing the bullies would leave Jimmy alone. "Have a good weekend with your tech stuff."

"And you," he said, "Have a good weekend, too. Perhaps if you need to write any assignments, you can come over and do them on my new system? It's got the new Windows Vista and Office 2007."

"Thanks, Jimmy," said Mel gently, "I'll bear that in mind."

Jimmy turned and seemed to have a skip in his step as he headed away. Smiling, Mel turned and headed up the corridor. She stopped at her locker and shoved her books into her bag. She kicked off her black leather school shoes and pulled out a pair of runners. She dropped the runners on the ground and slid her feet into them, smiling at the sense of freedom she felt when she changed her shoes. Stooping, she picked up her black leather shoes and dropped them in the locker. She slammed her locker shut and headed out the nearest door. The late afternoon sun was still hot as she skipped down the steps and headed off across the school carpark at a steady jog, relaxing into an easy gait. She ran towards the library, intending to pass it and head across the oval to go home. As she rounded the library, she skidded to a stop. Three boys stood in a semicircle around a fourth. Mel recognised the three immediately. Franco, Ben, and Jeremy. She had done well to avoid them for the months since the pool hall incident, and deciding this had nothing to do with her, she started to turn. That was when she recognised the fourth as Jimmy. He was bright red as if he had been running. He had hoped to avoid the three thugs waiting for him at the front gate.

"Try running, aye," Franco was saying, "I had detention because you dobbed. That pissed off my Dad. I didn't get my allowance last week as a result. I think you owe me."

"But I don't have money."

Jimmy's voice was pleading.

"Franco. Tell him about the poem." Ben's weaselly high-pitched voice cut across the pleading.

Jimmy looked suspiciously at the boys around him.

"Oh yeah. The poem."
Franco pulled out a bit of paper with a flourish.

"Sarah Mancini gave me the poem you wrote her. She wants me to read it over the school radio tomorrow. Dedicate it to you."

"How romantic," Jeremy cried out in a posh falsetto. He drew his hand across his forehead. "One feels one might swoon."

Jimmy looked like he was going to vomit.

"That's personal. She *gave* it?"

Franco had the paper open now. He started reading.

"The sun glows on high.

It is dimmed by your radiance.

Cold I am, alone."

"Cold, I am. Mmmm, Hehehe," Ben cried, mimicking Yoda from Star Wars. Jimmy stared at his shoes.

Franco stooped down to look into the boy's eyes.

"Sez thinks you're hilarious. She was pissing herself, thinking you thought you were in with a chance. Did you get Y fronts in the end? Dude, you couldn't get laid in a brothel."

The three of them laughed.

Seething, Mel realised she had not been noticed yet. She could slip away. And what? Leave Jimmy there with those thugs? Franco's fist flew and punched Jimmy with a sickening crack. Jimmy dropped to his knees with a cry, blood streaming from his nose.

"Pick him up," growled Franco, "it's time we taught him some respect."

"What goes on here then?"

The voice stopped the bullies. With horror, Mel realised it was her voice. She had a moment to ask herself what she thought she was doing before the three boys turned.

"Well, looky here. Our resident dyke," Said Franco with a grin. "I've been meaning to catch up with you. That cop saw my Dad. *That* cost me, too, dyke."

Mel's eyes hardened.

"Don't call me that."

"Whoa. Bitch got balls."

Mel bristled. Fixing Ben with a glare, she replied.

"Only compared to you. Leave Jimmy alone."

"Why?"

"'Cause I said."

"You?" Franco looked around, his smile broadening. He eyed her up and down. "You look good in your uniform. How about we talk about how you can compensate me for the trouble you got me into with my Dad?"

He reached out. That was when it happened. Dropping her bag, Mel stepped forward. Taking his hand, she pulled it over her. Taken by surprise, Franco stumbled forward. Twisting, using herself as a hinge, Mel ducked under the boy, pulling him over her shoulder and driving him hard into the ground. He gasped as he crunched down. Jeremy rushed forward. Mel caught the movement in the corner of her eye, turned and brought her knee between Jeremy's legs. He dropped. Gasping. Mel took another step forward. He grabbed Ben's jacket collar. She swept his legs from under him and slammed him into the ground, bringing her foot into his stomach. She turned back to Franco, who was scrambling to his feet. He launched himself at her. She ducked under his outstretched arm. Bringing her arm across his chest, she swept his legs from under him. He crashed back onto the ground. Keeping hold of his arm, Mel followed him to the ground. She turned his arm on itself and buried her elbow into his throat. All of this had taken less than ten seconds.

"No. Stay," she ordered, holding the forefinger of her spare hand up. The other two, who were scrambling to their feet, froze. Looking back at Franco, she leaned in. Through gritted teeth, he hissed.

"You're breaking my arm, you-"

Increasing the pressure on his throat with her elbow, Mel cut him off.

"I catch you bullying anyone else. You *will* need orthopaedic surgery to fix your arm. Got that asshole?"

Franco's eyes bulged, and he nodded vigorously, unable to speak.

She let go of Franco as she stood. She turned to Jimmy. Adrenaline raced through her body. Her heart crashed in her throat. Taking a couple of deep breaths, she settled her racing mind. When she took in Jimmy, she nearly cried out. He looked in pain, his hand pressed against his face. Blood oozed between his fingers. But there was something else. It took a moment, but Mel realised it was humiliation. Embarrassment. A girl had rescued him. She glared back at Franco, who flinched. She held out her hand.

"The poem."

He looked ready to protest, but she then thought better of it, slapping the crumpled paper into her hand. With a smile, she handed it to Jimmy before taking him tenderly by the hand and leading him to the school office. It was then that Hobson realised she wanted to be a police officer.

30/07/2020.

1850.

South of Tambo.

The first forty minutes had been tense. The only sound in *the Mutant's* cabin was the throb of the motor and the vibration on the road. Mick had tried to speak a few times to Akina about returning to Emerald, but she just scowled at the road ahead. Finally, he gave up trying and sat, staring into the red dunes around them. Eventually, Akina spoke quietly; the motor nearly drowned her voice.

"I'm sorry to be a pain."

Glancing at her, Mick replied.

"You're not a pain. I just want to know why you've come."

There was another brief pause.

"I needed to get out of home for a bit. Things are a bit tense."

"Why? What's going on?"

"It's just Dad. He's been difficult lately."

"How?"

Akina did not take her eyes from the road ahead as she spoke. The sunset bathed her with a red glow.

"I don't want to talk about it."

Mick's stomach leapt into his throat.

"Fuck he's not..." he did not know how to finish the sentence.

Akina looked at him, eyes questioning. Then, the realisation of Mick's meaning dawned.

"Not wha- No," Akina's eyes blazed. "Why the fuck would you- Why does everybody's mind go there?"

Face flushing, Mick looked helplessly at her.

"I'm sorry. I didn't mean to say...that is...the news is full of that sort of stuff. Apparently, it's on the rise with all the lockdowns. Look, I was going to offer help."

Akina's eyes softened a little.

"That's what my counsellor said," Akina's voice took on a falsetto "'Just making sure you're safe'. No, it's nothing seedy like 'that'," She said emphatically.

"Then what?" Mick's voice was small. Embarrassed.

"No. Look. Things have been tense. Dad wants me to go to university. In Kyoto."

Kyoto? Mick's heart leapt into his throat. Kyoto is in Japan. If she went there, he would lose her. What if she met someone else? He strained his memory, trying to recall if arranged marriages were common in Japan. Damn, for someone so attracted to Akina, he had not done his research. He realised Akina was speaking again.

"Well, for a start, I don't want to go to university. I want to be a mechanic, and secondly, if I went to uni, it would not be in Kyoto."

Mick felt more than a little relieved.

"Well, I get that bit. The bit about Kyoto. Your life's here in Australia. But why don't you do mechanical engineering? You got the smarts. You're top in maths and science at school."

"Because I love tinkering with engines. Cars. Fourbies. I want to take on Dad's business. But he says, 'It's no job for a girl. I knew I should have made you learn the piano instead of playing with cars," the last uttered with an impression of her father's voice. "He wants me to go to Kyoto. Learn accounting. Meet a nice Japanese boy..." she thumped the door with frustration.

"Wow. He was born in Australia, though, wasn't he? You'd expect him to be less...traditional," Murmured Mick.

"It's not like you and your mom don't have issues."

"What's that supposed to mean? Things are fine."

"Really. What did she say when you told her you were on this road trip?"

Mick sat quietly, staring out the window.

"You did tell her? Mick?"

"It's on my to-do list, okay."

Akina was aghast.

"Mick. She must be worried sick. She has no one else to go to. NO ONE. How could you do that to her?"

Guilt stabbed him. That was true. She was alone. He cleared his throat.

"Look, I've not had time. Things aren't great between us at the moment. Everything's a fight. I need to psych myself up. If I call her too soon, I won't say what I want."

"So, let me get this straight. You will risk everything to help some random internet stranger on the other side of the country, but you won't even call your Mom to tell her you're okay?"

"I...that is...look..."

"You're a piece of work, Mick. You're a great guy, but sometimes you can be a total dick?"

Mick stared for a moment. How did this become about him?

'So what did your Dad say when you told him you were running away with me?"

Akina blushed.

"That's different."

"How?"

"Dad has Mom and my brother. Your mom only has you."

"Look, I had no choice."

"Really. You were forced? At gunpoint?"

"No, of course not."

Akina cut in.

"There is no such thing as 'no choice'. We all choose our actions. You could have called her in several towns, but chose not to."

"I didn't choose not to...I forgot."

"And that's better, how?"

Mick stared at Akina, his mouth working, but no sound came out. He wanted to talk to his Mum. To say he was sorry. Apologise for being the idiot she had called him. But he needed time. It's time to have that discussion. If he rushed it, he would say the wrong thing. Start another fight. That's not what he wanted. What he wanted was to tell his Mum he was sorry. That he had been a selfish idiot; he wanted to tell her he loved her and tried to help her get the help she needed.

Now was not the time for that conversation. His eyes narrowed suddenly.

"Wait a minute. How did this become about me again? We were talking about you and your dad. Trying to make you go to Uni? In Japan?"

Akina winced. Her shoulders sagged. She sighed.

"Yeah. It's old-world crap. He's made all these decisions for me without asking me. We've been fighting about it for about a year. Things have become tense. I needed to get out of the house for a bit. Take a break."

Catching Mick's eye, she rushed on.

"That was my choice, though, and I own it. I see you as a friend. Someone who needs help. I also saw a way to escape town for a bit."

"But your Dad and Mum will *both* be worried. What you've done is just as bad. *And* I bet you haven't told them where you are."

Akina did not answer.

"Ha. Hypocrite much?"

"I've stayed out before. They're used to it. We argue. I have a tantrum and storm out. They rarely punish me when I get back. Fuck, they probably won't even notice I've gone."

"I bet they have. And this- " Mick waved his hand around *the Mutant,* "this could get you into real trouble. Christ, and make it more urgent for the cops to look for me. For fucks sake Akina. You've just illuminated the target I've painted on my back."

"Yeah? And? A criminal record could make getting a visa for Kyoto a bit difficult."

It fell into place. Mick looked at Akina.

"Akina, what I am doing is serious. Please don't risk it by *trying* to get caught."

"Yeah, Jack told me. You're trying to stop some old man from offing himself."

"Yes. An old man with a family who deserves to have him around. People like me who will miss him," Mick snapped harshly.

Akina looked abashed.

"Sorry, Mick," she said eventually. "I didn't think. I should have chosen my words better."

He sighed, taking a breath. After a couple of minutes, he said,

"All good. Just don't sabotage this. Please."

Akina sniffed, wiping her eyes.

"Look, I won't cause you problems, I promise. I'm along for the ride. That's all."

"And I'm glad you're here. It's a shame Jack's not here; he is always fun on a road trip, but he's on a bond. I didn't feel I had the right to expect that of him."

"Maybe you're not *all* selfish," said Akina with an appraising look.

Mick looked at her and nodded, looking back at the reddening dunes with a half smile. Suddenly, he felt his eyes getting very heavy. Yawning, he said,

"I'm gonna close my eyes for a bit. Wake me in two hours for my turn."

Akina nodded as Mick closed his eyes.

29/07/2020.

2015.

Tambo.

Hobson crossed the service station's forecourt. Her head was stooped, and she held her hat against the wash of the helicopter. With some skill in the ailing light, Naomi landed in the street in front of the service station. Their arrival was drawing a crowd. Not a lot happened in Tambo. A helicopter landing in the street would undoubtedly be spoken of for months, even years. Jessica came out of the service station door and met Hobson on the forecourt.

"What's all this? We don't sell Avgas," she shouted over the helicopter's din.

"Sorry for the disturbance. Senior Constable Hobson, Emerald Shire Police."

"Emerald?" Jessica asked, surprised to hear the name for a second time that evening—a surprise not lost on Hobson.

"This won't take long, ma'am. I am looking for a young man and a girl in a distinctive ute. Picture of a distorted kangaroo head on the bonnet. They are from Emerald. I understand he may have passed through here."

Hobson reached for her phone to show Jessica the photos, one of Mick and the other of Akina leaning against *the Mutant*.

Jessica's eyebrows nearly scalped her.

"Yes. I remember him. He was with a girl. She was Asian, I think. He filled up. They argued a bit and then headed down the Landsbourgh Highway, I think."

She gestured south.

"Argued. About what? Did she seem to be there against her will?"

"No, nothing like that, she was sitting on the bonnet when he came in to pay. Coulda run for it whenever. No, I don't think he wanted her around. He was askin' me about a bus back to Emerald. She wasn't having a bar of it, but. I'm not surprised. We only get one bus through, you see, and it doesn't leave until-"

"How long ago did they leave?"

Jessica's jaw clenched at being interrupted.

"Well, over two hours now."

Jessica looked at the helicopter and then back at Hobson.

"Should I be concerned? Are they, you know, infectious?"

"Oh no, nothing like that. They're breaking curfew, is all."

"Jeez. And the news reckons the police aren't taking shit seriously. What would you be sending after them if they were murderers?"

Hobson fixed her with a glare.

"You do not want to know."

Turning, Hobson leaned against the down draft as she returned to the helicopter. Her mind was racing now. Akina *was* with Mick. Willingly. Hobson barely knew her. She took this to be a good thing. Generally, if she knew a kid, it was because they had been in trouble. Not Akina. She had been aware of her, of course. Her relationship with Mick ensured that. But she had never paid much attention to the diminutive girl. What the hell was going on? What had prompted these two to...elope? Was that it? No. Not with the way she had found Mick and Twinkle tits last night. Hobson climbed back into the helicopter and gestured for the charts. Naomi passed them to her, puzzled. After Hobson's call cancelling their date, she had changed out of the blouse and skirt she had been wearing and was back in her orange flight suit. She watched Hobson examining the charts.

"Where are they headed?" Hobson growled, almost to herself. "Not Brisbane. They would have headed east from Emerald if they were heading for Brisbane. They headed west and then south."

Hobson's eye was drawn to the Queensland and New South Wales border. Was that it? New South? Why? Hobson traced her finger along the map. She needed to get ahead of them. Her finger rested on a dot on the map. The last one before the border. Cunnamulla. She leaned over to Naomi, tapping the map, and shouted.

"Can you take me here?"

Naomi looked at her fuel gauge. She ran through some calculations and then nodded.

"Sure. That's almost my range, though. I can't go much further."

Hobson grinned.

"I'll take you to Brisbane for a weekend away for this."

Strapping herself in, Naomi nodded, already powering up the engine.

Hobson could almost hear her say, "Damn straight, sugar," In her Southern United States drawl. As the Emerald Scenic

Experience helicopter flared, Hobson pulled her phone out and dialled Mr Sato's number. At least she had some good news after a fashion.

Mick could not see too much of the approach to Cunnamulla. Mick saw red sand on either side of the highway and nothing else beyond a sparse scattering of trees. Like most townships built up from cattle and sheep farming, the town had grown along the highway. Mick turned, driving up and down the high street, taking in a picturesque fountain and an old artillery piece near a roundabout. He turned to the left, following a road around, and as he passed over a bridge crossing a slow-moving river, he realised he had gone too far. A U-turn and another quick drive-through told him no service stations were open. He looked at his fuel gauge, noting with concern that his fuel was low. Driving out of town, back on the highway heading south, Mick laughed with relief when a roadhouse came into view, seeming to rise out of the ground. Its bright lights and flashing signs gave every appearance of being open. Turning into the roadhouse, Mick pulled *the Mutant* up beside a bowser. It was twenty kilometres south of Cunnamulla, a well-set-up place with a full washroom, café, and fuel. He had been surprised at first when he drove through Cunnamulla to find the petrol stations closed so early. Given the lockdown, he figured there was only enough business for the roadhouse, as no one was driving anywhere. And this was the country, after all. As he went through the town, he wondered if the streets at that time of night would be any fuller when there were no lockdowns. He figured there might be a few more cars around the local hotel. Otherwise not. He looked at Akina, who was starting to stir. He smiled affectionately as she sat up, looking around, blinking. As she wiped a little drool from the right side of her mouth, she looked drowsily at him and spoke.

"What are you grinning at? Where are we?"

He dropped his smile.

"Nothing. We're at Cunnamulla. The gauge has hit a quarter, so I figured we'd top up. They've showers, so I thought I might grab a quick shower. Wash off the shit from work. A bite of hot food. Coffee. Thoughts?"

Akina yawned and murmured.

"Sounds good. You're smelling a bit ripe. You go on ahead. I gotta put my shoes on. I'll meet you in there."

Mick gave a mock salute. As his hand was up, he took a discreet sniff of his armpit and snatched his nose away with a wince. She was not wrong. He climbed out of *the Mutant* into the heavy, warm night air. He looked into the wing mirror, rubbing his hand over the stubble on his cheek and chin. He needed a freshen-up if he was going to stay so close to Akina. Suddenly, he stood upright, giving himself a disgusted slap.

"OH, sure. A Shave. Put on deodorant. Some au de toilet. Why not a suit? A nice three-piece suit? Snap out of it. She's a mate. That's all," He muttered to himself. He took a deep breath and headed around to the bowser. The scent of the dessert was mixed with the smell of fuel and cooking from the roadhouse. The roadhouse was reasonably new, and the bowsers were digital, with small LCD screens piping news and adverts to the person at the pumps. There was a dusting of red sand covering everything. He lifted the nozzle, and his mind ran back to Akina. He grinned again, thinking of her tousled hair and the drool. She was never image-conscious, worrying about makeup and so on. To his mind, she didn't need it. She was usually neatly dressed, though. Even when working on engines, she said that workshops had to be tidy; otherwise, things would get lost, occasionally into the engines. He thought about her smile. Her dazzling smile as he teased him about how untidy he was. His mind ran to her eyes. Sparkly. Intelligent. Full of mischief. To see her so sleepy and drooly. He realised how beautiful she was, no matter what. He swallowed and tried to distract himself with the newscast from the bowser. Through the speakers, he could hear the reporter's urgent voice saying.

"...carry a face mask at all times and wear it outside your home. Unless you are alone in your car or with the members of your household, other mask exemptions include while you are eating or drinking at your usual workplace, where you can physically distance yourself if you are alone outdoors or with members of your household. If in doubt, wear a face mask. The impacted areas of Southeast Queensland include the City of Brisbane, Moreton Bay Regional Council, City of Gold Coast, City of Ipswich, ..."

Yawning, Mick ignored the voice as he looked around, wondering if there was anything else happening in the world. He began to take in other vehicles around the roadhouse. Three B doubles were parked and pulled up for the night at the truck stop. He could hear the nightlife chirruping away in the scrub beyond the pool of orange light the forecourt threw out. Beyond that, a couple of 4x4s were parked off in the darkness. He felt himself relaxing a little. It was peaceful here. The pump kicked, pulling him out of his reverie. He winced at the cost. This road trip was going to dent his holiday savings. But then, who knew when he was going on holiday next?

Moving to the back of the Ute, he lifted a flap and pulled out a small pack that held his wash kit. It was a simple affair consisting of soap, fresh undies, a T-shirt, and a towel. As he passed *the Mutant,* he tapped the window to wake up Akina, who was dozing again. He headed inside.

As he entered the roadhouse, he was hit by a blast of dry, frigid air. He called out to the man behind the counter, who was on his phone. The man stopped speaking as Mick walked past. He looked guilty.

"Probably not meant to be on his phone," Mick thought.

"Evening. Mind if I use the washroom?"

The attendant nodded. His three chins wobbled, flicking sweat over the counter. He watched Mick, who was headed out the back.

"Any chance of a pie and chips with a coffee? For two?" Mick called over his shoulder. The man nodded again. As he entered the washroom, Mick glanced back at the man. The man had not moved and was staring at Mick. Realising Mick was looking at him, he made it as if he were heading for the kitchen. Mick grinned to himself. The bloke had been on all night. He had the early morning stares.

"We've all been there, bro," he said to himself.

In the washroom, Mick looked in the mirror. He was covered in grime and smelled more than a bit ripe. He turned on the shower and undressed as it heated, the steam enveloping him. Rivulets of muddy water began to trickle down his back, turning into a torrent when he stepped under the blast of water.

Mick was not long in the shower. He breathed deeply, revelling in the heat. He adjusted the heat, turning it up slightly, and soaped himself. He looked down as he washed himself, getting a bizarre satisfaction in watching the murky water at the bottom of the shower morph slowly into clean water. A symbolic washing away of the troubles of his day. He washed his hair twice. Once to wash away the oil, sweat and grime, and once to make it soft. He stood, face turned into the stream for a moment, enjoying the feel of the water flowing over him. He was dragged back to reality by his stomach rumbling, a reminder he had promised *it* a treat, too. In the back of his mind, he began to imagine the ticking of a clock. Con. Cutting the water, Mick quickly dried himself with a towel and pulled on his clean clothes. Looking at his work pants, he wished he had packed clean slacks. At least his undies were clean. As his Dad used to say, when you travel, take a wash kit and a change of undies, and you'll feel a million bucks even if you can't find a shower. Mick could almost hear his Dad's voice. He smiled. Happiness quickly gave way to nostalgia, as thoughts about his father always did, pulling him into a dark mood. He quickly rinsed his grime out of the shower, leaving it clean for the next person and headed back into the roadhouse. It was jarring moving from the humidity of the shower into the dry, air-conditioned comfort of the roadhouse. So much so that he nearly missed Senior Constable Melanie Hobson leaning, arms crossed, on the corridor wall opposite the washroom door. Uniform immaculate. Reflective sunglasses and a blue mask in place. Mick's heart leapt into his throat.

"You've got to be fucking kidding me!" He burst out.

Akina had dozed off again as Mick headed inside. She had been dozing for about five minutes before she awoke with a start. Shaking her head, she ducked below the dashboard to reach for her shoes. As she sat up, she froze. A red and blue strobing light flared suddenly, and one of the four-wheel drives parked across the road moved across the highway onto the forecourt. Akina shrank into the seat as it passed within meters of *the Mutant's* bonnet, pulling right up at the entrance of the roadhouse.

"What the…" Akina's voice tailed off as the unmistakable form of Senior Constable Hobson stepped out of the car. Glancing at the seemingly empty *Mutant,* she walked into the service area. The man behind the counter gestured to the back, and Hobson headed out of sight. Fully awake now, Akina's mind raced. Adrenaline was a better kickstarter than any amount of coffee. They were in trouble. Mick, presumably, was still in the shower, so he would not have seen the police car pull up. This also meant Hobson would be out of sight for a few minutes as she waited for Mick. Akina looked at the attendant, whose eyes were glued on the drama unfolding, occasionally shovelling chips from an open bag into his stubbled face. Akina looked at the police vehicle. It was a Rodeo. Petrol. Not from home, she knew the Emerald Police vehicles from the workshop. It is presumably borrowed from the local police. Having helped her father work on them, she knew the type inside and out. Hobson had left the windows down. Akina had seen her take the keys with her. But the windows were down. This meant access to the bonnet release. Grinning, Akina opened the door and, crouching low, she sprinted over to the police car. She had a plan.

Hobson could not believe how easy things had been. The helicopter had landed on the Cunnamalla Urgent Care Centre helipad. After kissing Naomi goodbye with a reiteration of her promise of a weekend away, she pulled her mask back up and stepped away from the machine, which powered back up. As she waved, the muscles around her eyes softened. The helicopter rose. With a deep breath, Hobson turned and headed towards the small team of healthcare professionals rushing to meet her. The helicopter headed back north with a roar. Glossing over her off-duty status, it had been a couple of minutes to explain her presence to the welcome party as the helicopter engine faded. The medical staff took her quickly through the motions of ensuring she was not unwell or from a hot zone. By this time, the police arrived and took her to the local station. Hobson quickly drew up a plan with the local police. Initially reluctant, they went with the plan when she promised they would not need to worry about paperwork. Figuring Mick would need to fill up soon, she consulted a map of the local area and dispatched the local police constable to ensure the other stations were closed. She left the roadhouse twenty kilometres out of town open. Hobson then requisitioned a police 4x4, which, according to the local Senior Constable, needed a run anyway. She headed to the roadhouse to speak to the clerk on duty. For his part, Josh, an unshaven, morbidly obese man in his forties, had been easy to convince. He also told Hobson he was single. His mother lived with him, not the other way around, and he was studying online to be a security guard. He informed Hobson he had wanted to be a cop himself but had failed the entry exam twice. Hobson was not surprised. With his assurance for assistance in place, Hobson withdrew to the other side of the road. She pulled up behind a bush to conceal the police car's reflective tape and waited. Another car pulled up nearby, and the driver got out and set up for a night's sleep. It was about nine-fifteen, and she soon dozed off. Her phone buzzed just past ten. She sat bolt upright. It was Josh, the roadhouse clerk. She looked across at the forecourt and saw the ugly but familiar shape of *the Mutant* at the bowser. Kicking herself for her lack of discipline, her eyes were drawn to Mick. She watched him through the roadhouse windows as he headed out the back. She looked back at *the Mutant*, eyes narrowing. Empty. Presumably, Akina was already in the shower. Smiling, she started the motor, fired up the lights and rolled over to the roadhouse. Soon, this would all be over.

And so there Hobson stood, enjoying Mick's stunned look as he stepped through the washroom door. He was enveloped in sweet-smelling steam. The water had flattened his ridiculous mullet.

"You've got to be fucking kidding me!" He burst out.

"Mind your language. And where's your mask?"

"How?" exclaimed Mick, ignoring the question. Right then, he had to admit a grudging admiration for Hobson. "I mean...how? What are you? A Terminator? Why can't you just leave me alone?"

"To what? Elope with Miss Twinkles back there?" Hobson gestured to the ladies' washroom.

"No. What? Elope?" Mick shook his head. "Who's eloping?"

"Don't try to pull that. Her Dad is beside himself with worry. Your mother's already stressed out, you selfish prick, and you pull this shit. I'm taking you home before you drop yourself in real shit."

Mick tensed. Straightening, Hobson readied herself. She recognised when someone was preparing to run.

"I can't. I need to keep going. This has nothing to do with eloping. Akina wasn't even meant to be here. A friend needs me," His voice had taken a desperate tone.

"Right. A *friend* needs you," Hobson made air quotes at friend; "You? Pull the other one. Who would turn to you for help? You need to get your own shit sorted before you try to help others. What about your mother, you selfish prick? Do you have any idea what you're putting her through?"

He looked away for a moment, shoulders slumping. He looked back at Hobson. He looked so lost. For a moment, she softened, missing the bond she and Mick had once shared. He used to call her Aunty Mel.

"Mum doesn't care. If shifts are filled at work and the house is clean, she's happy with a bottle. She's probably glad Dad's gone. She probably thanks you for not stopping him. With me not around, there are fewer people to clean after."

'Not stopping him,' his words were like a punch to her guts. Not for the first time, she was glad of the glasses and mask she hid behind. Pressing her hand to her thigh, she made a fist. Her mouth barely opening, she spoke in a tone almost a hiss, carrying the fury laden with guilt his words had sparked.

"Right now, you can be thankful for the CCTV in this shiny new roadhouse because if we were ANYWHERE else, you would have copped a slapping for that."

Josh, scratching his bulging midriff with his left hand, flicked a switch with his right. He called helpfully out from the counter.

"CCTV has had a temporary 'cut in power.' Go for it."

Hobson glared at the man behind the counter.

"Shut it, tubs!"

Josh shrugged. He reached over the counter and pulled a packet of chips from the specials bowl. He opened them. Reaching in, he pulled out about half the contents of the packet. With a shower of crumbs, he shoved them in his mouth and began to munch. Despite this cop's attitude, this was still the most interesting shift he had had in a long time.

Looking back at Mick, Hobson continued.

"Your mother and I had no control over what happened. She 'fills shifts' so you don't lose your house. So, you can eat and play big boy in that *thing* out there. She works *hard* so you have a future. It is because of the sacrifices she makes, because of what she has been through. I have been trying to keep you out of fucking trouble. Because of what I missed, what I should have done with your father, I am trying to take you back with as little fuss as possible. I owe it to your father. He was like a father to *me*. He covered my ass many times."

"Really?" Mick was sceptical. Hobson frowned. "Cock blocking me last night. Was that for Dad's sake? Pulling me over every five minutes is for Dad? Waiting for me outside of a dunny in the ass end of nowhere...to honour Dad?"

"Someone's got to."

Straightening, Mick met her glare. That lost boy was gone for now. He spoke after a tense pause. As he spat the words out, however, he wished he could stop himself. Knowing he was stepping over a line.

"You're not Mum's type, you know. She won't jump into bed with you out of gratitude."

This time, the fist flew. Josh gasped excitedly, spraying chips over the display as Mick dodged the punch. Hobson punched the wall through the plasterboard with a crack and split her knuckles on the stud. The stud buckled. The plasterboard fell away from where, a second ago, Mick's head had been. With a roar, Hobson glared down at her deformed fist, blood oozing over the knuckles. Mick ducked around her and sprinted for the exit of the roadhouse. He could see Akina had moved *the Mutant* next to the police 4x4. Skirting around Hobson's four-wheel drive, he slid over *the Mutant's* bonnet. Mick ripped open the passenger door. Before he was settled in, Akina pressed her foot on the accelerator, and the vehicle lurched off.

Wincing, Hobson nursed her hand as she approached the clerk, staring at the departing 4x4. Akina had been in *the Mutant* all along. Kicking herself for being careless, Hobson decided that she must be tired.

"That didn't go as planned," he observed. Josh turned suddenly pale and looked like he was going to vomit at the sight of Hobson's bloody hand. The remainder of his chips sat in his hand, forgotten. Looking up from her hand, he shrank under Hobson's glare. For the first time in his very comfortable life, he understood what the term 'feeling his testes shrivel' meant. In a quieter voice, he squeaked, "That little shit didn't pay."

Hobson awkwardly pulled out her wallet with her left hand.

"What was his bill? Emerald Police will pick this one up."

"Oh. Okay," said Josh. He rang up the bill. Clearing his throat, he asked, "Do you want me to press charges?"

Taking Hobson's card, he busied himself with facilitating the transaction.

"No. I will do that as a police witness," lied Hobson.

Josh nodded. After an awkward moment, he said,

"Cool. Well, good luck bustin' his ass."

Josh handed Hobson's card back. She gave a tight smile as she stuffed the card into her wallet. She turned and headed to the door of the roadhouse. Over her shoulder, she said,

"The speed my rig can go; luck does not come into it."

"I thought you were gone," said Akina as she moved efficiently through the gears.

Mick looked behind, waiting to see the police lights fill the road house.

"Yeah, well, Mel's buttons are easy to push. You have to hit the right topic, and she loses her shit."

He turned, looking anxiously behind.

"C'mon, floor it."

"It's all good. We'll get ahead of her. What topics?"

Mick's jaw clenched. He felt terrible about what he said. He did not like hurting Hobson. They had been close once. Deciding to ignore the question, he looked behind again.

"Faster," Urged Mick, looking at the speedometer. "Hobson will catch us."

"Eighty kilometres an hour in this rig, with this engine, will give you more economy. Therefore, fewer stops. Therefore, covering more distance." Said Akina.

"But Hobson's car is a cop car. With cop mods," he added, seeing he was not getting through. It can go faster than us."

"I doubt it," smiled Akina, tossing something on Mick's lap. He picked up the component in his hand.

Hobson glared under the bonnet at the engine.

"She took the rotor arm. Clever girl."

She could not help but admire Mick's friend. She was too good for him. Letting the bonnet drop, she looked up at the departing lights of *the Mutant,* now a red smudge in the dusty darkness. Hobson turned and headed back inside. Josh was wolfing down a meat pie over a plate with a second pie and a big pile of chips. He looked at her with surprised guilt, swallowing hurriedly.

"Back so soon?"

Hobson arched her eyebrow at the meal. Josh flushed.

"Couldn't let 'em go to waste."

Pie crust blew from his mouth as he spoke. Hobson stepped back, wincing. This man was truly revolting.

"I'm afraid there is more waste than there needs to be around here."

"Huh?"

"Never mind. Nearest mechanic. NOW."

Established on the 6th of June 1859, the border between Queensland and New South Wales is about 3339 kilometres long. Travel between the states used to be simple enough, but in 2020, it was classified as a hard border. Police checkpoints were dotted on all the main roads, preventing travel between the states. At one of these checkpoints, Constable Andrew Thorne was bored. He looked at his watch. It was just past one on a clear night. Another forty minutes, and it was his break time. He stamped his feet, rubbing his gloved hands together and looking up at the expanse of stars, losing himself for a few moments in the feeling of insignificance he felt whenever he looked up at night. Tearing himself away, he checked the flashing strobe beacons lining the road, warning drivers to stop. He had to admit, as he looked up and down the empty highway stretching off in both directions, he felt redundant. Steam seeped out from gaps around his mask, and not for the first time, he regretted the tuna pasta salad he had had for a snack. He would have taken the mask off, but he was expecting a visit from his inspector at some point and did not want to give the man another reason to reprimand him. A fit man in his mid-twenties, Thorne had been a member of the police service for nearly eighteen months now. He had grown up on reruns of *The Bill* and *Blue Heelers,* shows in which the investigations, followed by the thrill of a chase and an arrest, appealed to a young Thorne. But he loved the interrogation. The battle of wits between the crim and the cop. This had been his inspiration to join the police. As he stood there stamping his feet to stay warm, he concluded policing was not what he had expected. Instead of being a member of the Tactical Support Group, here he was manning a border crossing, stopping travel between New South Wales and Queensland. It was not exactly the high action he had anticipated, growing up on a Die Hard diet and Lethal Weapon viewing diet. There was a saying amongst the cohort of officers at the outpost. "Bored at the border". Then he saw a halo of light crest a distant hill heading towards his post. After several minutes of watching them approach, he had to admit the lights were impressive. The road suddenly went dark as the vehicle pulled over, the lights switched off, leaving a purple dot in his vision. Suddenly alert, Thorne could make out standard headlights in the distance. He reached for his radio.

"Sarge?"

"What!"

The caravan housing the "HQ" was about two kilometres back down the road.

"There's a vehicle up the highway, about a kilometre. It appears that the driver has spotted us and is having second thoughts. Should I check it out?"

There was a pause, and the sergeant said without changing his bored tone.

"Do whatever you like. Let me know if they have a deck of cards."

"Join the police, they said. It'll be a fast-paced challenge, they said," Muttered Thorne as he headed to his car.

Akina nearly drove straight into the roadblock. The car's motion, Mick's breathing, and general fatigue had dulled her wits. As she pulled abruptly to the side of the road, she reached down and flicked off the driving lights. The clock on the dashboard glowed 0120 at her in green numbers. Mick awoke with a start. He rubbed the sleep from his eyes.

"What's going on?" he asked, wiping saliva from his mouth.

"The border's up ahead," Akina replied. "It's blocked. Probably crawling with cops."

"What? Now?" asked Mick, who was now fully awake.

Akina nodded.

"Let's swap spots."

Akina nodded, and they awkwardly slid around each other, Akina over the top and Mick underneath. They paused, Akina's hands resting on both seats, pinning Mick in the middle. Their eyes locked. Mick wanted the moment to last forever. Then, with a cough, Akina moved to the passenger's seat. Mick slid into the driver's seat and looked at the GPS attached to the dash.

"I'm not gonna ram 'em..."

"You're not telling me you haven't considered this part," Groaned Akina.

"I... that is... I... no."

A car detached itself from the grouping of flashing lights and headed their way.

"We had better not stay here too long," Mick muttered, dropping the car into gear. In a flurry of gravel, he pulled the car in a tight arc and headed back in the direction they had come. As they moved around the bend, he looked up into the mirror and saw red and blue strobes start to close the gap between them.

"FUCK," He snapped, pushing the accelerator. *The Mutant's* engine roared, and the car lurched.

"What?"

"Cops wanna chat."

The modified 4x4 engine whistled slightly as the wagon sped up. Mick knew he only had seconds before the Police realised he was running, and then even *the Mutant* would be no match for the power of a police car. Suddenly, Akina lunged across the cab and grabbed the wheel. With a squealing of tyres, the Ute tilted dangerously, veering to the right.

"What the?" yelled Mick as the vehicle crashed through a gate into a field. *The Mutant* spun out of control as Akina's hand flashed out and deftly twisted the end of the indicator light lever, killing the headlights. The vehicle stalled as it stopped spinning and sat facing the road, rocking violently. Mick sat for a moment, hyperventilating as the Police car, its driver now realising he was in pursuit, rocketed past, sirens blaring. Moments later, the dust from their diversion floated across the highway. Mick sat, gazing at the blur of lights as they receded into the distance. His head snapped to look at Akina, who was sitting in the passenger seat, wide-eyed and breathing heavily.

"WHAT...THE...FUCK...AKINA!"

"Sorry. I saw the gate and..."

Mick swallowed a few more times before his heart rate slowed. "Next time. Please. Just say stop."

Akina nodded. He looked around, suddenly aware that the ute was at an angle.

"I'd better check the wheels are still attached."

As Akina nodded, Mick grabbed a torch from a bracket above his head. He climbed down and made his way around the wagon, shining the light on the wheels, brow furrowed. Sure enough, a tyre had popped off the rim.

"Dammit."

Akina jumped out, joining him. She looked at the tyre.

"Ouch."

"I gotta spare, but it'll take ages to pull out. By the time I-"

"We don't need the spare. Grab your jack and compressor. I got this," She grinned.

Thorne glared ahead.

"Dammit," He hissed. Somehow, the 4x4 had evaded him. Suddenly, a set of lights appeared above a rise ahead of them. He made out a four-wheel drive speeding towards him. The speed radar alarmed. He looked at 140 km/h. Well, he at least had this driver for speeding. Then, an idea hit him.

"Really?" He muttered. "The old U-turn manoeuvre."

Keeping his lights flashing, he angled his car across the road. Thorne climbed out of his car and leaned against the bonnet with his arms crossed. To his surprise, red and blue lights began flashing as the vehicle slowed down.

Hobson arched an eyebrow at the sight ahead. A police vehicle, lights flashing, was blocking the road, a young officer leaning against the bonnet. Slowing with a tight grin, she reached down, flicked on her own red and blues, and pulled up. She wound down the window and looked at the officer, who was now standing, looking confused.

"Want to get that shit heap out of my way, Peewee? I got perps to catch."

Ignoring the barb, Thorne snapped upright.

"Where are you from?"

"Emerald."

"A bit far off your patch."

"As I say, I'm pursuing a couple of perps."

"Did you see a 4x4 with powerful lights go past you back there?"

Hobson was suddenly interested.

"Powerful lights? Fill me in, kid."

Mick lifted his tarp and rummaged around the back. He pulled out his jack and, with a grunt, his compressor. Akina, meanwhile, had gone to the passenger side, reached into her backpack, and pulled out her deodorant. Mick was busying himself jacking the back of the car to give them access to the wheel. Akina grinned.

"Good. Get the compressor ready to roll," she said, kneeling. Mick watched as she jiggled the tyre into place and then proceeded to fill the gap between the tyre and the rim with deodorant.

"What are you doing?"

"Fitting your tyre."

Akina pulled out a lighter and ignited the deodorant. With a deep pop, the tyre popped into place around the rim.

"Don't just stand there. Pump her up."

Hobson drove down the road slowly. Behind her, Thorne sat not more than three meters off her rear bumper. She reached for the mic of her radio and snapped, not taking her eyes off the road.

"Thorne, if you're not a haemorrhoid, get off my ass."

Thornes's voice crackled back.

"We are in pursuit. Why aren't we going pursuit speed?"

"If you don't back off, I will personally back this rig over the bonnet of your pissant sedan and park it on your throat. You missed something in your rush before, and...ah, there it is."

Her eye caught it, a mist of dust over the road. Her eye followed it to the remains of a gate to the left. She swerved her car and pulled in short of the gate. Hobson reached down and flicked on her floodlights. Thorne pulled up in his low-slung pursuit car. Leaving the engine running, Hobson climbed out and looked at the scene in front of her. She heard Thorne hurrying to catch up as she made her way across the dry ground, feet crunching in the dust.

"What's that smell?"

"Deodorant," said Hobson.

"What?"

Stopping, she knelt and examined the churned soil. She could see what had happened. The gouges in the earth. The imprint of the jack and...and the deodorant. That old trick.

"Dammit," She hissed, looking at the tracks heading southeast. "Thorne!"

"Yes."

"Get on the radio, let your superiors know there is a 4x4, olive drab..." she paused. She should say that she called the Mutant, rego MUT004, and broke into NSW. You are looking for a young man named Michael O'Hare and a girl of Japanese descent named Akina Sato. Both are 17 years old. Instead, she carried on. "Tell the NSW police. Olive drab 4x4, no other details yet. I will follow the tracks here in case they break down again. We are close."

Mick eased *the Mutant* along. He was aware time was ticking past, but he was driving with his lights off as less than two hundred meters to his right was the road. Five minutes ago, they had passed the New South Wales side of the police block, and now he was looking for a gap in the fence line. He was confident he had little time before the police officer in the car realised they had been tricked. Mick just did not know how long. The road had started veering to the left, meaning this area was now blocked from the view of the police on the border. Shrugging, he applied a little more power and pushed through the wire fence. He eased *the Mutant* embankment, pulled onto the New South Wales Road, and continued South.

Mick gazed at the road ahead. They were making good time now. They were about one hundred and eighty kilometres from the New South Wales and Queensland border. He had to admit he had not expected to make it this far. He had thought that the Police from the border would have certainly caught him. Every kilometre he made, the more uneasy he became. Why had they not been caught? He had voiced this question to Akina, but she had just shrugged. Akina had become quiet. She looked at Mick.

"Do you like her?"

Mick looked at Akina, ripping him from his thoughts about potential pursuit. Residual unease from his thoughts made him suspicious about this random question.

"What? Who?"

"Leanne. Do you like her?"

He had not expected this conversation thread and would have given anything to be elsewhere.

"What do you mean *like*? I guess. She's nice. She's smart-" he knew he was rambling, but he needed to bring his mind from his thoughts into this conversation. Akina had a mental head start after all.

"No idiot. You two fooled around the other night. Do you *like* her?"

"Fooled   around?"

"You know what I mean," said Akina, raising her eyebrows and nodding.

"We didn't do anything."

"Really?" Akina could not keep the half smile from her lips. She was relieved, if not a little sceptical. Mick focused on the road ahead.

"Really. Hobson stopped her."

The smile dropped. "Hobson stopped *her*?"

Mick nodded. "Leanne was really in a mood to...you know. I didn't want to. Then Hobson turned up like she always does and...well...interrupted us. If I'm honest, I was kinda happy to see her," He finished weakly.

"If she hadn't?"

Mick suddenly felt very hot. He switched on the air conditioning. He did not want to be here.

"I don't know. I wanted to...I don't know."

Akina turned the air con off.

"Fuel consumption. You don't know?"

"Well," Mick cleared his throat. "Well, I...that is she...I couldn't stop her. She was on me, and I didn't want to...I don't know...hurt her feelings? It's dumb, but I felt backed into a corner at the time. Now I'm like, I should have told her to back off. But then she was a little sad. Lonely. Needing closeness. But I don't do that sort of thing. I'm saving myself for...I don't know."

"That's so lame. 'Saving myself?'" mimicked Akina, incredulous.

"Yes," Said Mick, suddenly defensive. "What's wrong with that? These days, a bloke's gotta be careful who he…you know…with. I don't want to go into casual flings and have people claim shit I didn't do or that I made promises. So, I'm saving myself for someone I trust. Like. You know? Really *like*."

"So, you didn't…you know. Do anything with her?"

"No. Well, we kissed. That is, she kissed me. Like I say. I got confused."

"How so?"

Mick paused, choosing his words carefully. He was glad for the darkness, which was hiding his hot face.

"Look. Leanne *is* hot. True. All the guys at school wanted to…you know. Or her sister. Or both. Okay. I get *that*. She's smart and feisty. Funny," Mick grinned, "I mean, she took Hobson to…"Akina had started to glare again. "Never mind. I just don't feel we…we…well, click. She doesn't like camping or fourbies for a start. With her, it would've been just…I don't know; it was a night of fun, I guess. Not even a night. An evening. But like I say, nothing happened."

Staring at the road ahead, the red sand of the embankment deepened with the sunset. He switched on his lights, and the trees and bushes lining the embankment were bleached into the harsh world of blacks and whites as the sun finally dipped below the horizon, turning dusk into night. Concentrating on the road, Mick did not see Akina press her face against the window. The engine purred, the only other sound to the riff of ACDC.

"Is there anybody you do like?" she asked after a while, her voice lighter. Less angry.

"Angus Young?" he grinned awkwardly, glancing at Akina. "Do you know why he wore a school uniform on stage?"

"C'mon. I'm serious. Who's the lucky person?"

This time, Mick paused. He gazed ahead at the ghostly forms of trees lining the embankment on the side of the road, not seeing. He could feel the pulse in his throat, which had suddenly gone very dry. His mind raced, drowning out AC/DC's Back in Black. If he said something and she liked him, they could work something out. If she did not want him, though, then the next couple of days would be awkward, maybe the next couple of months.

"Mick?" Her voice was suddenly uncertain. Nodding his head, he made a decision. He looked at Akina. Their eyes locked, hers wide with anticipation, his wide with panic. He could feel his heart pounding in his throat. He felt sick. As Mick looked across at her, all sound faded. He could hear nothing, not even the engine of *the Mutant*. All there was Akina and him. Alone.

"Actually, I," he cleared his throat. Why was it so dry? "That is…, er, I like-"

They collided with something on the highway. *The Mutant* lurched with a resounding crash. They cried out as something rolled over the bull bar, cracking the windscreen as it flew over the car with a squeal. Mick locked on the brakes. They were both thrown forward against their seat belts. *The Mutant* veered off the highway, ploughing off the road and over the embankment and coming to rest on the other side of a red sandy dune. They sat, gasping. The sound of the

Mutant's suspension springs creaking broke the silence as it rocked. When the rocking stopped, there was silence.

"What the fuck?"

Akina's voice made Mick jump. Shaking his head, he looked at her.

"Are you okay?"

"What the fuck?"

"Are you hurt? Akina, look at me. Are you okay?"

Akina looked at Mick, eyes wide as saucers. She breathed heavily. After a couple of moments, she nodded.

"I think so..but what the fuck?"

"I don't know. It happened too fast. I think I saw a shape about six feet tall roll over the bonnet. A hitchhiker?"

"What was a hitchhiker doing on the road at midnight during a lockdown?"

"Who else could it be?" He stopped gazing into the settling dust. "Police? Trying to wave us down?"

Their eyes locked, this time in panic. Mick grabbed his torch from its bracket and pushed the door open. His heart had been replaced by his stomach in his throat.

"Fuck no. Fuck no. Fuck no. Akina, grab the first aid pack from the back," He cried, his voice choked with dust as he climbed out of the Ute and scrambled over the dune to the road. Stumbling down, he looked at the way they had come. Through the dust, he could make out a writhing form on the highway's edge.

"Hello?" he called, moving slowly towards it. It occurred to him that the police had guns. Shooting someone who had just run you over could be forgiven. His torch cut an almost solid beam in the cloud of dust. The figure had stopped struggling, but he could still make out a rise and fall of its chest. He coughed to clear his throat and then called again.

"Hello?"

He made his way towards the body. It cried out once more and then went silent, unmoving. Mick edged forward, keeping his torch on it. The dust cleared. He suddenly laughed with relief as Akina ran up to join him, first aid pack in hand. They looked at the mangled kangaroo in his torchlight. She let out a relieved laugh.

"Is it dead?" she asked.

"If not, it ain't happy?"

"Sorry, Skip," said Akina with genuine feeling.

Mick's legs suddenly became weak. He moved over to the embankment and sat down. Akina came to join him. They both sat, breathing heavily. Eventually, Mick stood up.

"We'd better get moving. God knows where Hobson is right now."

He held out his hand, and Akina took it. He helped her up. She held onto it, and they both derived comfort from each other's touch.

"C'mon," said Akina. Holding hands, they moved back over the embankment and looked at *the Mutant* wheel arches buried in the dune.

"Ah, crap," They both groaned in unison.

"Your tyres will not have the grip for this one."

"I've got her booked into Bergs next week," said Mick reflexively. The comment reminded him of the conversation he had with Hobson. He glanced nervously toward the highway. The dune hid them, but she noticed everything.

"Let's get to work," muttered Akina as she disentangled her hand and moved back to *the Mutant*. For a moment, feeling the loss of her touch, Mick stared at her as she moved efficiently around the rig. Lifting hatches, she pulled out recovery gear, shovels and the air jack. He always marvelled at how well she knew his Ute. Mick's Dad had bought it for him five years ago. First, they had just played around with it together and then had begun to tinker with it. That tinkering evolved into upgrading and modifications. Akina had always been fascinated by vehicles, wanting to apprentice at her father's service station. Despite her lack of years, she was among the few people he trusted under *the Mutant's* bonnet. She moved around the back, lugging out the heavy recovery kit. Stopped and grinned at him.

"Are you waiting for the police to come and help us or what? You recover. I fix. That's the deal, remember."

Glancing toward the road again, Mick grinned as Akina began to dig into the sand under the front wheels. Moving to the back of the ute, he dropped the tailgate to reveal the rear-mounted winch. Pulling the controller out of a side compartment, he plugged it in and extended it.

Freeing *the Mutant* was a time-consuming but straightforward affair. Once they had dug around the tyres, Mick wrapped the winch cable around a nearby tree. They winched the Ute slowly from the sandbank with the vehicle in reverse. As Mick packed the recovery gear away, Akina moved around the vehicle to inspect it. She was muttering to herself as she went. Finally, she lifted the buckled bonnet. In the light of the torch, she examined the engine. When she was finished, she dropped the bonnet down with a clang. She pulled some rope from the recovery kit and used it to secure the bonnet. Whilst Akina was doing this, Mick pulled out his phone and opened Grouplink. There had been no new messages from Con. Given the time of night, he had not expected any, but he still wished there had been at least one. He could almost hear a clock ticking as they worked. Mick considered sending Con a message, but thought better of it. He did not want to give the man a reason to move his timetable forward. While they were working, they heard a couple of cars speed past. He could not tell if either was Hobson, as the embankment hid the road. But it made him uneasy. After about forty minutes, Akina started *the Mutant*. The engine coughed into life with a shudder. She stepped out.

"I think we are going to be okay. But don't push her too hard."

"Will she manage the embankment?" asked Mick.

"She has to," Said Akina, crossing her fingers. Mick nodded. So, with Akina as lookout on top of the embankment, Mick edged *the Mutant* up and over the bank back on the side of the road. Akina moved to the driver's side.

"I'll drive for a while. You need a rest."

Mick nearly argued but thought better of it. He moved over to the passenger's side. Moving into the driver's seat, Akina wiggled the gear shift and eased the ute onto the highway. Mick checked his phone; there were no new messages.

"I think she's in good shape, but I suggest taking it easy from here on," She said to Mick after a few moments of driving. "Some new tapping sounds are coming from under the hood, I'm not happy with."

Mick nodded, his jaw cracking with a yawn. He relaxed back into the seat, not for the first time, thanking his lucky stars for Akina's company on this trip. He looked uneasily at his watch.

"How fast do you think she can go?"

"I'd not push it too hard."

"It's just that I think we are behind time now. We can't afford any more delays. I don't think we will make it to Frankston as it is."

Akina nodded. "I know, but if we push her now and blow something…"

"Yes, but it's just that I still haven't had a reply from Con. What if we're too late?"

"What is your plan when you get to Frankston?"

"How do you mean?"

"I mean, what are you going to do? Knock on the door and hope he's happy to see you? What if you are too late?"

Mick gazed at her.

"Oh, for fuck sake. Are you tellin' me you've not thought that far ahead?"

"Yes. No. Maybe. Look, I'm just goin' to talk to him," Said Mick.

"Talk? What if he's dead?"

"I'm hoping he's not."

"Hope. That could work." Muttered Akina.

"It might," Mick reached behind and took his jumper off the back seat. "Look, I'm getting some shut-eye. Wake me in a couple of hours."

Akina nodded. Mick balled the jumper into a pillow and put it between his head and the glass. He was asleep within minutes. Akina glanced at him. As he started to snore, her smile became troubled.

30/07/2020.

0450.

Cobar.

Akina pulled *the Mutant* into the petrol station. She nudged Mick awake. He jerked up mid-snore.

"What's up?"

"You top up. I want to give *the Mutant* a proper once-over in decent light."

Mick nodded. He opened the door and slid out of the passenger seat, stretching. He could feel the cartilage in his spine and neck crack as he slowly rotated his upper torso and windmilled his arms. With a yawn, he headed around to the fuel side. He unscrewed the cap and began filling up. In the meantime, Akina moved around to the dented bonnet and untied the rope. The bonnet hinges screeched as she lifted it. Her wince faded as she frowned at the engine. She reached in, wiggled hoses, and checked connections. Pulling out the dipstick, she checked the oil level. She was relieved that there was no leak, so she unclipped the air filters and tapped out the sand and dust. Finally, she checked around the radiator for leaks. Nodding, she dropped the bonnet with a thump and fastened the rope back in place. After tying it back down, she crouched, looking under the car. Brushing herself off, she was suddenly aware of Mick standing beside her, offering her a cola and saying, "Attendant says it's been a dead night. We are the first people he's seen. That means no Hobson."

Akina held her hand, "I'll grab that in a moment. I have to go powder my nose."

Mick looked at her blankly as she headed to the service station. She looked back over her shoulder and laughed at Mick's expression.

"I need the dunny."

"Oh," Mick said. As he watched her walk away, Mick pulled his phone out and tried to call his mother. The phone rang out. Once again, he was relieved, but concern began to edge its way in. Why was she not answering? Akina was gone for several minutes. Mick took the road trip notes out of the glove box and examined them. He ran through the maths in his head. It was going to be tight. His gut told him they were not going to make it. His only hope was Con's call. He wondered if Con's son was a talker or had loads of kids. Maybe they would keep Con talking. He looked up as the door to the service station opened. Akina walked briskly towards him.

"You know," she said, "I reckon by the end of this trip, you'll be able to write a travelogue about the servos between Emerald and Frankston."

He grinned, "It's been a fun tour; it would be good if other places were open, you know, to mix it up a little. We'd better get moving. I've been doing the maths. We've fallen behind schedule."

Akina nodded. "I was wondering that myself. I looked up the route on my phone while I was...busy. It's a good nine, ten hours or so."

He offered her the cola, which she took with a smile.

"You need to drink more water," she said, leaning against *the Mutant next to him*. The bottle hissed as she opened it, and she took a deep swig.

"You sound like my Mum. How's *the Mutant*? Is she up to it?"

"Yeah, she seems okay. A bit of crap in the filters, but otherwise, she's in good shape. Don't push her, though. She's been through enough for her maiden voyage."

Mick nodded, frowning.

"That might be hard. Ten hours with Hobson after us, we have to push it to stay ahead of her. Assuming she's not already ahead. Anything could have passed us when we were off the road."

Akina nodded and took another swig of her cola. She let out a small belch.

"Nice one," Mick said reflexively. They tapped bottle ends as a toast.

"Thanks. I've been thinking about that. I bought us some time back, pulling the rotor arm. How about I hang back here? If Hobson stops here, I fuck her motor up royally."

"What? You're staying here? No. No way."

Akina held up a hand.

"Hear me out. I'll hide up here. If she doesn't turn up, I'll catch the train to Sydney, then Brisbane, then Emerald."

Mick gave her a long look.

"You'll head back home? After all, you said? You don't intend to stay somewhere else? Like Sydney?"

Akina looked away.

"No!" said Mick firmly.

"I-"

"No Akina. I don't want you to leave. We both have stuff to sort out, and running is not how to deal with it."

"Says you. Have you spoken to your mom yet?" Akina glared at him. "How dare *you* tell *me* what I can do. I've had enough of that from Dad without you starting."

"That's not fair. I intend to go home as soon as this has been sorted. You are talkin' about…leaving. You call me selfish? What do you think running away will do to your parents? They'll worry. I'll worry about you…I'll miss you."

Akina looked back up at Mick.

"Really?"

"Yes."

Akina broke into a big smile. She took a swig of her cola, thinking.

"OK. Rethink. Though, for the record, I did intend to head back to Emerald."

Mick nodded sceptically, not quite believing her.

"What makes you think she'll stop here anyway?" he asked.

"She must. To see if you've passed. If she's behind, she'll pull in here. If she's ahead, she'll come back."

"I'd prefer a plan where we stick together. I've kinda liked having you look after me. And *the Mutant* will miss you," smiled Mick.

Akina blushed, "I still would be looking after you, just in a different way. And I'll be spending a lot of time with *the Mutant* when you make it back to Emerald."

"I never thought I could be jealous of a fourbie."

Smiling, Mick looked across at the clerk staring at them through the window. He could feel the minutes sliding away. He had to admit that the more he thought about it, the more Akina's plan had merit.

"How would you have fucked up her engine? I got sugar in the back."

Akina grinned.

"Oh, Mick, my naïve pupil. *That's* a myth. Depends on what she's driving, but I'd have thought of something."

"Are you sure you'd 've gotten back home, okay?"

Akina looked at him sharply, sensing he was wavering.

"Yes. I looked it up on my phone. I hide over there in the church doorway. If she turns up, I tinker with her motor, hide again, and catch the train to Sydney tomorrow. From Sydney to Brisbane. Brisbane to Emerald."

Mick looked at her thoughtfully.

"It could work."

Akina nodded. Mick suddenly felt ashamed he had considered her plan.

"No Akina. You'd be here by yourself-"

"Mick. No! It's the only way. She will keep coming at you unless she can be stopped."

"What if she doesn't come this way?"

"Then we've lost nothing. Sometimes, you have to roll the dice."

"I don't like this, Akina."

Akina's eyes flashed.

"Yeah, well, it's *my* choice. You're taking your risk for a good reason. Let me take mine."

Mick paused, looking helplessly at her.

"Does the train travel to Melbourne?"

Akina shook her head. "Covid restrictions. Melbourne's locked down. They're calling it the ring of steel. Good luck getting through that, BTW."

Mick foundered. She held Mick's eyes unwaveringly.

"You can only stop me with cable ties and duct tape. How'd that one look?"

Realising he was not going to win this, Mick nodded.

"Look, if you run into strife, call me, and I'll come back."

Akina smiled, nodding.

"Whether you're an old man in Frankston or a young lady in…" She looked around, seeing a sign on the door of the service station. She continued, "Cobar. Mick O'Hare to the rescue. I have to say, I've really enjoyed our first date."

Mick looked at her, struggling to follow the conversation.

"What?"

She reached up, pulled his head down, and crushed her lips onto his. After a stunned pause, he moved closer, wrapping his arm around her waist and pulling her in close.

Fifteen minutes later, Mick was driving down the highway on his leisurely journey. He touched his mouth, Akina's lingering kiss still burning his lips. He knew he was grinning stupidly. He tried to stop but couldn't. He wanted to go back. Pick her back up. Spend more time with her, and continue the moment. For once, something looked like it would go his way, but she insisted he carry on. Images of Akina in trouble kept flashing through his mind. Akina is being arrested. Akina is stranded in Sydney. Akina not returning to Emerald, instead leaving to pursue her own life. That was the one which worried him the most. What if this had all been a plan to run away? He shook his head to clear it. His jaw clenched with a mix of regret and determination as he drove on, his lights cutting through the darkness. Up ahead, he saw headlights appear on the horizon. Dropping his drive lights, he instinctively looked for a side road. Spotting one, he turned the car slowly.

"I'm not suspicious. No sudden moves, just a guy on the way home at four in the morning," He mumbled to himself.

He pulled around, facing the intersection he had just turned through. He parked to the side and switched off his lights. Waiting. Two cars flashed by; one was a police four-wheeler, and the other was a dark sedan. His breath caught at the sight of the police fourbie. Hobson? If so, another near miss. Then it hit. Hobson would be coming from the opposite direction that Akina expected. He pulled out his phone. No signal.

"Damn, Akina, please be careful," He said as he pulled *the Mutant* back through the intersection and continued on his way.

Mel walked through the back corridors to the carpark where her 2002 Ford station wagon sat. She smiled contentedly, for tonight, she had a date with her TV. Season 3 of Babylon 5, a massive bag of corn chips, pizza and a good part of a slab of cider. Lost in this thought, she missed the sound of footsteps behind her. Not until two pairs of strong hands grabbed her arms and yanked them behind her did she realise she was being followed. She was dragged to the right into the men's locker room and dumped on the floor. She winced at the smell of stale urine and deodorant. She stood, rubbing her shoulders. Mel looked at the two constables who had dragged her in, Beyer and Price. Seeing those two, she was not surprised when, seconds later, Williams entered the locker room.

"So, you snitched," He said with no preamble.

"That kid was cuffed and restrained. You didn't need to keep punching him," Replied Mel.

"Yeah, well, because of you Ethical Stand-"

"Cry me a river. If you hadn't beaten a cuffed prisoner, they'd have never heard of you."

Williams looked at his two friends, giving them a shrug. In a flash, William's fist cracked into Mel's jaw. She was able to twist and avoid most of its impact. But she still stumbled and fell.

"Stay down bitch," snapped Williams.

"Why do thugs always hang around in groups of three?" she asked.

"We're meant to stick together, cover each other's arses. How can we trust you after this?"

"Cover each other. Not cover up for each other."

"Shut the fuck up, you dumb dy-"

"I wouldn't finish that sentence if I were you. I might be thinkin' you were a bigot."

The voice came from one of the toilet cubicles.

"You didn't check the stalls?" groaned Williams.

A toilet flushed. There was a pause while the occupant delivered a hacking cough before the door opened. Out stepped Sergeant Jerry O'Hare.

"Ah fuck," Said three voices in unison.

"Indeed," Murmured O'Hare. He moved to the sink, washed his hands, dried them on some paper towel and then moved into the circle, putting himself between Mel and the three constables. During this time, no one had moved.

"You see, I can't abide bullies in the uniform. You are the lowest form of scum on earth. Three on to one. That's not even close to brave."

He was met by silence. The three officers shifted awkwardly, not meeting his steady gaze. He turned slowly, briefly catching Mel's eyes. She gave the slightest of nods. He winked at her before turning back.

"However, I can't help but feel that if this isn't sorted today, it will fester like a decubitus ulcer."

Williams, Price and Beyer looked at him blankly.

"Google it. But as I say, this is going to bubble on. So I propose this. Williams versus Hobson. One on one. Looser resigns."

"I'm in," said Mel straight away.

Williams looked incredulously at O'Hare and then back at Mel, against whom he stood a good head and shoulders above. A sly smile crawled across his face.

"Cool. Right. I got it. Cheers sarge. Where? When?"

"Here. Now," said Mel, seeing the look on Williams's face, she added, "Unless you're a soft cock."

Williams looked at O'Hare, who raised his hand, stepping back.

"All I'm going to say is be careful what you wish for, Williams," He said.

Mel looked at O'Hare and opened her mouth to speak when a fist crashed into her face. She dropped again.

"Thanks, sarge," Said Williams, rubbing his fist as he turned away.

"For what?" asked O'Hare, "It's not over."

He pointed behind Williams at Mel, who was getting to her feet. She could feel the blood running from her split lip. She spat bloody saliva onto the floor. The blow had not been direct; she had managed to roll with it, giving the impression of a knockout punch; she still felt a little lightheaded.

"My turn...bitch," She smiled.

William's gazed at her, astonished.

"You want more?"

"I hope that wasn't all you had, or this will be a short fight."

Williams looked at his friends, who shrugged in response. They, too, had never been in this position. Shrugging, Williams moved in with another direct punch. Mel weaved around easily enough. She closed the distance. As she brought her knee in between Williams's legs, she brought her hand under his chin. Williams was lifted off the ground, propelled backwards, and crashed against the lockers. He slid to the ground, rolling into the fetal position. Mel stepped over his vomiting form as she headed out the door. Grinning O'Hare followed her. Stopping to kneel, he said to Williams, "I expect your resignation to be on my desk tomorrow. And you two, clean up this mess."

O'Hare stood and hurried out after Mel.

He caught up with her in the car park. Breathing hard, he asked, "Is that out of your system now?"

Massaging her jaw, Mel looked at him and grinned. The grin slid away as she noticed for the first time how thin he had become. His skin had greyed.

"Yup. You think the other two will be a problem?"

"No. They'll sharpen up once he's gone. They're not beyond redemption. Good practice for the nationals in two months."

Mel nodded, "You okay, Sarge? You seem a little out of breath."

O'Hare smiled. "You sound like Mickey. I'm okay, just out of shape. Too much time behind a desk."

He gave another hacking cough. Mel nodded sceptically. O'Hare looked around, reached into his shirt pocket, and pulled out a folded envelope. He offered it to Mel. On it, in her precise writing, was written;

'Sergeant O'Hare; Emerald Police Service.'

"You still want to resign?"

She looked at the letter, reached for it and paused.

"I don't know."

"Look, the service is full of bullies and corruption. If all the good cops quit, think of what would be left. You made a stand today, and the service is better for it. Thank you. I'm proud of you, Mel."

She reached for the paper, paused and then took it.

"Look...I'm only where I am because of you. You know that right?"

"Bollox. You're a good cop."

"I know that," She missed his wry smile. "What I mean is that night. When you stood up for me in the alley, it was the first time anyone had...backed me up. Not even Dad. He just called me a...you've always been there. In this town, it's lonely to be different."

"I know. Try being an Irish cop," O'Hare smiled.

"My resignation after that night on patrol with Williams; you're the only reason it took me two weeks to write the letter. I didn't want to let you down."

"You haven't. And as long as you keep doing what you are doing, you never will."

Mel opened her mouth to speak and then closed it for a moment, thinking. She wished she knew how to say he had been more of a mentor in her life than her 'father'. Instead, all she could say was, "Low blow. But thanks."

He grinned.

"We're having a barbecue tonight. Fancy coming for some grilled meat? You can bring Naomi. I know Mick'll love to see you again."

Nodding, Mel said, "That'll be nice. Cheers. I'll need to check in with Nom. I'll text you and let you know."

O'Hare nodded, turned back, and limped away.

Across the road from the service station, Akina watched from the doorway of the small church. She had been crying; her decision filled her with guilt, but she needed to get away from her father. This had been the perfect opportunity. She felt terrible about lying to Mick. She had realised tonight she genuinely loved him. But the chance to leave Emerald and start a new life wherever she liked. It was too good to pass up. She was looking up the road when she heard a motor coming behind her. She shrank back into the shadows of the doorway. Her breath caught as Hobson pulled up next to a bowser. Akina watched as Hobson climbed out and headed up to the cashier's office. She did not even look tired. She gave the police officer a few more moments and sprinted across the road. The rotor arm trick was good, but not permanent enough. Loosening the oil sump plug would do the job properly. Crouching, she watched the entrance. She could see Hobson. Back at the door, she was speaking to the clerk. The clerk looked surprised that a Queensland police officer was this far south of the border. Clutching the adjustable wrench she had taken from *the Mutant,* Akina crouched and moved around to the driver's side, using the Rodeo as cover. Heart thumping, she slid under the vehicle. Reaching across under the vehicle, she began to loosen the plug with slow, rhythmic turns. It came loose suddenly, and black oil poured from the hole. She grinned as she wriggled out from under the UTE. Looking across, she could see the cashier nodding and pointing down the road Mick had taken. Jaw clenched, feeling nauseated, Akina moved to the back of the vehicle. Keeping the bowser between her and the service station's shop. She backed away slowly towards the church. Hobson was still speaking to the clerk. There was a crunch of gravel behind her. Firm hands grabbed her. She dropped the wrench as she was lifted and slammed against the side of the truck. Winded, she gasped as she stared in confusion at another Queensland police officer. His grinning face inches from hers, he spoke in a cool voice.

"Got'ya."

Gripping her by the back of her neck, Thorne dragged Akina the length of the 4x4 and slammed her face down across the bonnet. She felt cuffs biting her wrist as he snapped them on. She wanted to be sick. Factoring arrest into a plan was one thing, but when it happened...she looked at the pay booth. Hobson was pushing her way through the door, grinning in triumph.

"Good work, Thorne."

"I can't believe they tried the same trick again, but I don't think I got to her in time," said Thorne, frowning at the oil beginning to seep from under the four-wheel drive and across the stained concrete.

Hobson glared at the container, then back at Akina.

"It's all good. He left here about forty minutes ago. We should be able to close the gap in your interceptor easily enough."

Hobson gestured to Thornes' V6 Stinger parked two hundred meters up the street.

"Chuck her in the back, and let's go," Said Hobson as she walked over to lock up her 4x4. "We're close now."

Akina struggled as they dragged her to the police car.

"Stop struggling, and I'll take the cuffs off." Snapped Hobson.

Akina looked down, began to walk meekly, and was bundled into the back of the Stinger.

Akina massaged her wrists. Thorne started the car as Hobson climbed into the passenger seat, giving him back his cuffs.

"They didn't need to be so tight," she said.

With a screech of tyres, Thorne yanked the wheel hard, and they took off down the road. Akina sat in the back, glaring at Hobson.

"Who's your friend Hobson?"

"Constable Thorne," Thorne answered. "South Queensland Highway Patrol."

"Bit out of your jurisdiction, aren't you? I mean, last I checked, the Queensland police weren't federal."

"Yeah? Well, sometimes you gotta do what needs to be done," snapped Hobson.

"All this because of your vendetta with Mick."

Thorne looked at Hobson.

"Personal? I thought you didn't know him."

"That's what you assumed, kid."

Akina smiled, sensing a weak link.

"He's young for a cop. Your career might survive this cross-border stuff, but will his?"

Thorne looked nervously at Hobson. With her jaw clenched, Hobson turned slowly to look at Akina. Lowering her glasses, she met Akina's eyes through the partition between them.

"You so want to shut the fuck up right now," she said slowly.

Ice played along Akina's spine as she met Hobson's stare. She shrank into her seat and took Hobson's advice. Hobson turned to look at the road ahead. After a couple of moments, Akina pulled out her phone and began to type a message.

Mick watched as the police car rocketed past. Mick glimpsed the unmistakable form of Hobson on the passenger side, eyes fixed on the road ahead. He saw Akina slumped in the back. Mick did not recognise the driver. The car disappeared into the distance. He looked at Akina's message on his phone, which had arrived in a rare moment of reception.

I stuffed it. There are two of them. Find cover.

They are in a highway patrol interceptor.

They'll get you if you don't hide.

Mick had been puzzled at first. Who had Hobson teamed with? But in the end, he decided to hide. He had pulled off the road into a small copse of eucalypts and waited. Mick stared down the road, giving them five minutes. He felt no small amount of guilt. First, because Akina was in trouble because of him, but second, because of the moment of relief he felt when Akina was caught. Knowing she was safe. He considered staging a daring rescue but decided against it. Hobson knew who she was and would pick her up again at home. Besides, Mick could not shake the sense that Akina had not intended to return home. It had occurred to him that he had never heard Akina describe Emerald as home. This made him uneasy. Home. While he had reception, he picked up his phone and tried to call his mother again. It rang out. This made him worry. After a moment, he dialled Jack's number, and on the fifth ring, he picked up. In a tired voice, he drawled.

"Whoever this is, it had better be good."

"Hey, dude, it's me," Mick said.

Jack sounded suddenly alert.

"Hey, the fugitive calls. Look, I tried to deflect Hobson; I'm not sure she's convinced."

"Yeah, nah, she wasn't. Our paths crossed a couple of times tonight. She has Akina now."

"Fuck. How'd that happen?"

Mick quickly updated Jack on what had happened.

"You've been busy."

"Have you seen Mum at all?"

"Yeah, she's lying here next to me. Why would I have seen your ma?"

"I've been tryin' to call her. She's not answering. I was wondering if you'd drive over and make sure she's alright." "What? Man, do you know what time it is?"

"Course I do. I'm just worried."

There was a pause, and for a moment, Mick thought Jack had fallen asleep.

"Jack?"

"Alright," Jack muttered.

"Cheers, I owe you one."

"Only one?"

Jack broke the connection. Mick smiled as he started the engine and eased the ute onto the road. He had been feeling wrong about how he left things with his mother, thinking he needed to make changes. He had been able to ignore the nagging thoughts, but now realisation slammed into him. Akina was right. Here he was, risking everything for a man he had never met; in the meantime, he had barely spared a thought for his mother, who had given so much to make sure he was okay. He glared at his reflection in the windscreen.

"You *are* one selfish prick. Dad would've been so ashamed. This was not how a man of the house should be," He muttered.

First, he decided to make sure his mother cut the number of shifts she worked. She needed a break. If he spent less on his car, he could give more to her, and she could cut back on her work hours. He smacked the steering wheel several times, each contact punctuated by an emphatic

"Fuck!"

He blamed his Mum for all the time she spent at work over the past few years. But Hobson was right. All that time was spent keeping the house so they would not lose what she and his father had built together. The house was his mother's connection to his father. Suddenly, the road in front blurred. He wiped the tears away. Next, he would help her get support. Sure, it was easy for him to judge her for drinking. But she was only trying to forget what had happened with his father. Now he thought about it. He had been burying himself in his car, trying to deal with his father the same way. He had been so focused on his own pain, he had missed…no…ignored his mother's. The road ahead continued to blur, and he wiped away tears.

The wind howled outside, banging the screen door at the front of the house. Tilda awoke with a start in the grey light of dawn.

"Michael?" she called out reflexively, looking around. Blinking the grains of sleep away, she was confused for a moment. She had fallen asleep on the couch in her scrubs. Midnight Oil's *Blue Sky Mining* was still playing on the stereo. Other than that and the wind, the house was quiet. She looked at the clock. Then she remembered. Mick was on the loose somewhere in Queensland, according to her last contact with Hobson.

"Time for bed?" she mumbled, standing up. Her foot kicked a CD case, which she picked up and put back on the coffee table. It was *Midnight Oil's Greatest Hits.* Tilda looked at the clock and shook her head.

"Nope. No peace for the wicked, Tilda. Time to get ready for work," She corrected herself. Moving around the coffee table, she kicked something else on the floor. Looking down, she saw the framed photo of Jerry on his academy graduation day, resplendent in his police dress uniform. She remembered she had been hugging it before the vodka had sent her to sleep. She picked it up gently.

"Sorry about that. Good morning, ye idiot," She said with a sniff.

She kissed the photo, her lips barely brushing it, before placing it in a cabinet drawer.

She turned the stereo off. She did not have much time to get to work. Looking down at her scrubs from the previous day, Tilda considered skipping the shower, washing her face, and tidying her hair. She sniffed the scrubs and winced. No amount of deodorant would cover that. She had spilt vodka over herself last night. Rebuking herself, she stumbled out of the front room and into the kitchen to put the kettle on. She must remember to change and shower when she got home in future. She shuffled through the house to her bedroom and checked her phone for messages. She raised her eyebrows, seeing six missed calls from Mick. She was about to ring him when there was a knock at the door. Vexed, she walked to open it and was surprised to see Jack. She looked at her watch.

"Did you wet the sleeping bag? What do you want this time of the morning? Aren't ye meant to be camping with my son?"

Jack winced, rubbing the back of his neck as he often did when he had been caught up to no good. He tried to ignore the strong smell of alcohol.

"Ah, hi, Mrs O'Hare. This is awkward. Mick's been trying to call you. You've not been answering."

"Really? Can ye blame me? Look at the time," snapped Tilda.

"Er.   I   guess   not."
"What's he up to, Jack?"

Jack looked like a rabbit in headlights.

"Who?"

"The Pope. Who do you think, ye idiot?"

"Oh. Mick. He's up to nothing. Why?"

Tilda fixed him with a glare.

"That is, he's not up to nothing. Obviously, I mean, none of us is ever up to nothing. I mean to say that even when we are in bed, we are up to sleeping. So...you know."

Tilda's glare softened, her shoulders slumped.

"Please, Jack. I need to know. I've already lost my husband. Is my son about to run away?"

Jack's insides twisted. He looked at the bleary-eyed woman in front of him. The script he had been rehearsing vanished from his mind. Shaking his head, Jack decided Tilda had been through enough. She deserved the truth. No face-saving spin.

"No. No, of course not," He looked around, wishing he was anywhere but here at this point. He looked around at the thrashing trees on the nature strip and then made a choice.

"I'll tell you what I know."

"Come in. You make the coffee. I'll ring work, tell them I won't be in."

Jack entered the house and moved to the kitchen, filled the jug and set it to boil water. After a few minutes, during which he pulled out two cups, he found the coffee, milk and sugar. He added some coffee and sugar, poured in milk and then stirred in the hot water. He could hear Tilda's apologetic voice as he walked through to the front room. She rang off and looked at him with a sigh.

"I don't like leaving them short, but when I told them Mick's disappeared, they understood."

They sat down, Jack in an easy chair and Tilda on the sofa. Facing each other. Eyeing the open Midnight Oils CD cover on the table, Jack began.

"Do you know of Con?"

Tilda shook her head slowly.

"I know the name. Friend of yours and Micks, isn't he? A mechanic or something?"

"Kind of. After Jerry…left, Mick was lost." Jack looked at Tilda. "You both were. Having *The Mutant* in the garage kept him thinking about Jerry."

"Well, it is…was a tough time. Jerry was never far from any of our minds."

"True. But they had that plan, him and Mick, to fix her up. You know. *The Mutant.*"

Tilda sighed.

"Jack, is there a chance you can crack on with this story?"

Jack swallowed, standing up again. Mick was going to pay for this.

"I'm tryin' too. But it's complicated. You see, Mick nearly sold her. *The Mutant.* But he couldn't shake the idea Jerry wanted to rebuild her with him. That's why Mick found a 4x4 forum on Grouplink. He had met a fella there. Con. Mick said he was a bit of a laugh. Loves Fourbies. Always givin' advice to people."

"On how to fix 'fourbies'?"

Jack nodded, missing the bite in Tilda's voice. He carried on.

"Well, Con and Mick clicked. I think Con became...like a fill-in father for Mick, not in a creepy way. He helped Mick through the rough times by getting Mick to focus on the rebuild."

Tilda nodded.

"Mindfulness through working with your hands can be therapeutic, but I fail to see..."

Jack held up a hand, nodding his head.

"About three months ago, Mick thought something was off. He said the messages were NQR. He couldn't say what. They were shorter. Less happy. Stopped talking 'bout his wife and family. Not unfriendly. Just...short. At first, Mick thought he'd pissed Con off. Mick can be like that. You know? Like the time he made that joke at the-"

"Jack," Tilda's voice was sharp. Jack jumped as her eyes narrowed. "Where is Michael?"

"New South Wales. Heading into Victoria," Jack blurted.

"He's going where?"

"Melbourne. Victoria," Jack's voice tailed off.

"I know where Melbourne is. Jesus wept. The idiot. All that way, by himself.

Jack laughed nervously; Tilda rubbed her eyes, struggling to put all this together. The hangover had arrived, and her head was pounding.

"Why in the name of Jesus is he heading there?'

"Con's messages," Said Jack. He looked at Tilda as though that explained it. Tilda rubbed her eyes with a sigh. Sometimes, when taking a patient's history, you listen to what you assumed was irrelevant. This looked like one of those times.

"OK, Jack. Sorry, I interrupted. Please enlighten me. Why did this…Con's messaging upset Mick. What did he say?"

"Nothing, to Mick."

"JACK!"

Jack paused; he did look like he wanted to be elsewhere.

"If you just let me finish a sentence, I might get there," He said defensively.

"Again, sorry, Jack," the words were squeezed between clenched teeth.

"Mick read Con's comments to other people. He saw that Con was like this to everyone. A few folks had asked Con if he was okay, but he never answered. Mick asked if everything was okay. Con even ignored him. Then, yesterday morning, Con sent a message that seemed like a…well, Mick reckoned a goodbye. He was worried. He's headed to Melbourne to see if Con needs help."

Tilda stopped rubbing her eyes and stared.

"Why'd you not go too?"

"I offered, but he wanted me to cover for him. He's gone with…"

"Who?"

"Akina."

"Akina? Servo Akina?"

"Yeah."

"But I've sent Hobson after him."

"Wait? What? That was you?"

"I didn't realise. I thought he was running away. He's been so impulsive. Like his Dad was at his age."

"It's okay. He's been able to dodge the Terminatrix for now."

Tilda's eyes flashed.

"Look, you show Mel some respect. She might seem hard, but Jerry's leaving left a hole in her life, too, you know. I think he was her mentor and her best friend in this town. She was there for us when he…went…making sure we were okay. Keeping an eye on Mick."

Jack's temper flared.

"Perhaps if *you*…" He cut himself off too late.

"What?" asked Tilda.

"Never mind."

"C'mon. Out with it, ye little gob shite."

Jack sighed. He was in now. Him and his big mouth.

"Look. It's not my place, I know, but perhaps if *you'd* been there rather than the Term-er Hobson. Perhaps if you weren't working so much, Mick would not have had to rely so much on a stranger on the internet."

Tilda went bright red, her mouth working to form the words. But then she suddenly stopped, looking deflated. She reached across, opened the drawer, and picked up the photo of Jerry again, gazing at the handsome man in the police uniform. She looked at her reflection in the glass. At the aged, grey face, sagging under the eyes. Her red hair had once glowed, but now... Suddenly, it hit her. Jerry would not want this. He'd hate to think he had caused her this much pain.

"I'm sorry, Jack; you're doing your best. To be honest, you've been great for Mick. Keeping him out of trouble. Con. Hobson. I suppose I've relied on them too much to do *my* bit. I've been telling myself I've been working these hours to make ends meet. Honestly, I don't need to work so much. It's just...easier to hide at work...or in a bottle."

Jack looked around the room, unsure of how to respond. She looked at the photo of her husband in her hand. She caressed it, chasing the line of Jerry O'Hare's grinning face.

"Jerry was always noble. Helping others. He saw himself as a knight in shining armour. Old-fashioned. That's why he became a cop. That's how he met Mel. That's how we met."

A tear dropped onto the glass of the photo. Reaching across, Jack grabbed the box of tissues off the table and offered them to Tilda. He looked away as Tilda took one, wiped the glass first and then her eyes. It was a private moment. She sniffed.

"It was nearly thirty-two years ago, to the day we met, ye know."

She did not look up from the photo. Jack looked around for an escape. This was heading towards an emotional conversation, and he didn't like those much. Finally, resolving that Mick would pay for this, he shook his head.

"You must've been..." his head furrowed, trying to guess her age. "Twenty-five." He settled on confidently.

Tilda's head snapped up.

"Twenty-five? Ye cheeky fucker. I was sixteen. D'ye know how we met?"

Jack shook his head, not daring to answer.

"He saved my life. Can you believe that now? Him, seventeen years old. Risked everything to save me. *That's* where Mick gets it from. Not able to turn away from someone needing help. Do you have any idea what kind of bond forms between two people? Jerry 'n me. Mel n' Jerry. Mick n' Con. When they step up to help you when you feel alone. You never shake the thought you owe 'em that. But to Jerry, it was just what a man did."

Jack shook his head again, knuckling back a sudden tear. He was suddenly unable to speak. What was it with this family? Their emotions just drew you in.

"A helluva story, I can tell you. You wouldn't believe such happenings could occur here in Emerald. I used to be adventurous. I read too many Famous Five and Secret Seven books. I wanted an adventure. But be careful what ye wish for aye."

Jack nodded; his shoulders slumped in resignation, but Tilda did not seem to notice.

"I was born in Belfast. That's Northern Ireland, in case you were wondering."

Jack wasn't.

"Ma' and da' they wanted to escape the troubles, see. So we moved to Australia when I was eight and to Emerald when I was sixteen."

"Troubles?" Jack asked.

Tilda looked at him for a moment.

"Yes. Well, if you aren't aware of that one, I don't have time to explain it to you now. Where was I? Ah, yes, sweet sixteen. New in town. Dad used to encourage me to learn all sorts of stuff. He'd say, 'Tildy, to develop as a person, ye need to step outside ye' comfort zone.' So he'd have me out running, rock climbing. He taught me navigation by the sun. It was fun in its way. It meant I was thought of, as they called us back then, a 'Tom Boy'. When we moved up from Sydney, see, we just up and left. Came out here. What an adventure in itself. I was a runner. Running helped me relax. I was out for a run one night…I saw…some people. Bad people they were. It was July 28th 1989. It was windy. Like this morning. I remember that because I was having second thoughts about going for a run."

28/07/1989.

1845.

Emerald Botanical Gardens.

The July evening was windy. Clouds scudded across the moon, occasionally darkening the shadows within the shrubs and trees of the Emerald Botanical Gardens. Tilda Buchanan ran, stepping artfully between ruts made by car wheels and leaping low-lying hedges. She was in the zone, not running a set route but randomly picking points and running to them. Breathing heavily, she looked at her watch. She was setting a good pace. A sound carried through the wind, which brought her to a sudden stop, a snatch of hushed conversation. It came from somewhere off the track along which she had been running. Seeing nothing, she was uncertain what to do next. The voices carried again. This time, she caught words. The accent that hit home. Familiar. She did not know of any other Irish families in Emerald back then. Frowning, she edged forward. The sensible thing would be to ignore that niggle of curiosity, turn and start running back the way she had come. But where was the fun in that? She was quietly confident that, as a star runner in the interschool cross-country team, she could outrun anyone in the gardens. She *had* resolved not to be held back by what she was told she should and should not do. Push herself out of her comfort zone. Hence, she was running at night through the botanical gardens of a new town. The wind whipped branches against her bare legs as she moved off the path and edged through the scrub. The spark of curiosity took hold, becoming a burning need to know. The scrub ended, and she came to the edge of a small clearing. She moved around until she found cover. She could feel her heart beating in her throat. Staring into the darkness, she could see nothing. Tilda crept further forward. Crouching. She moved a branch for a clearer view. At first, she saw nothing. Closing her eyes momentarily, she hoped to improve her night vision. Opening them again, Tilda peered deeper into the clearing. Her breath caught as she saw the backs of two men, their dark coats making them patches in the darkness. The branch Tilda was holding snapped. Tilda dropped to the floor. Her heart pounded as the two men whirled around. Whipping out hunting knives, they advanced towards where she lay. Tilda held her breath, praying furiously. But breathless from her run, she could not hold her breath for long. Lights were dancing in her eyes, and her fingers were tingling when she let out an explosive gasp. Two pairs of eyes locked on her, and with a speed at odds with their size, they moved across the clearing. With a desperate squeak, she scrambled to her feet but was not quick enough as strong hands in an iron grip locked onto her arms. Tilda let out a cry. One of the men cuffed her on the side of the head. Her head swam as the men pulled her up and began dragging her across the clearing. The world steadied around her, and she began to fight, kicking her legs in the dirt and trying to shake her arms free.

"Knife. Mask. You boys are a bit early for Halloween."

The voice cut across the clearing, stopping the two men. They turned, dragging Tilda around to face the dark stranger. One of the men let go of Tilda and fumbled for a moment in his jacket. He pulled out a torch. Switching it on, he pointed it at the figure. The boy, who was lit up, blinked at the sudden light. He was tall, but he did not look much older than Tilda. He was dressed in a school uniform and carried a bag.

"What the fuck is this. A creche. Do kids not stay inside anymore?"

The voice of the man with the torch was jarring in the silence of the night.

"Trick or treat, smart arse."

The second man snarled in a heavy Irish accent as he lunged. Tilda cried as the boy swerved around the arc of the knife into and under the man's arm. He crouched as the man moved over him, and the boy straightened. The man crashed into the thick, prickly acacia bushes nearby; he yelled as he tried to break free from the thorny branches that gripped him. The boy turned, moving cautiously toward the other man. The shorter man gave a sudden yell as Tilda, momentarily forgotten, dragged her heel down his shin. He reflexively let go to grab his shin. She turned, giving him a hard push with both arms. He toppled backwards. The boy reached Tilda, who arched an eyebrow at him.

"Run," Snapped Jerry. He grabbed her hand and headed back onto the path at a run.

Yanking her hand away, Tilda called as she shot past him, "Don't need to tell me twice."

Tilda burst out of the bushes, followed closely by Jerry. They vaulted the gate, taking a moment to catch their breath. They looked up and down the empty road. They could see houses in the distance, but otherwise, nothing.

"Where to...now?" he gasped.

Tilda shook her head, chest heaving.

"Well, I live...about 800 meters...up the road," the boy gestured up the street.

Tilda nodded. As they began to move, a figure dropped from the gate, landing behind them. He grabbed Tilda from behind and held the hunting knife to her throat.

"Right, now. Let's stay calm. Follow me into the park," Growled the man, not seeming out of breath. He was the taller of the two men.

"Look," said Jerry, "I bet you're a nice bloke, but we're *not* following you in there."

A car turned onto the street. The man glanced up the street; Tilda stood frozen. Wide-eyed.

He opened his mouth but was cut off by a sudden blue strobing light and the throaty roar of the V8 Holden Commodore motor as the police car lurched toward them, siren blaring.

"Shit," In a blur, the man was gone back over the fence, leaving Tilda and Jerry to sag to their knees slowly. Tears were streaming down their faces.

"....and that was how I met Jerry O'Hare. There's a lot more to that story, but it was from that he got the taste for the police work. From there, we were inseparable for nearly thirty years. Till things got too much for Jerry, and he left...Now Mick's gone adventuring...like his..."

She sighed, eyeing the half-bottle of wine on the coffee table.

Jack had sunk on the couch next to Tilda, and he was transfixed. Mind racing.

"Far out. Did you ever find out what those men wanted?"

"Oh yes." Smiled Tilda. They gazed at the photo of Jerry, Tilda's mind still decades away.

Jack's mind crashed back to the present.

"Look...I am sorry 'bout all this. But...Mick? What now? I mean, when you think about it, you'd expect Mick to take off like this. You know, to stop this bloke from...well, you know. He didn't want to hurt you."

"But he did."

"Yeah, but...well...you have to admit, Mrs O'Hare, you've been a bit of a bitch yourself lately."

Jack looked meaningfully at the wine bottle on the table. Tilda glared at him and then looked down at her feet. They sat for several minutes like this, with Jack looking awkwardly around the room. Shoulders straightening, Tilda looked up.

Her eyes, bleary and tired a few moments ago, are now alert. With a curt nod, Jack said.

"Righto. Here's what we do. We call Mick. We tell him he's an idiot. We let him know I'm okay and that he can come home when he's done."

Jack nodded, grinning with relief. He looked again at the wine bottle lying on its side on the table.

"Tilda," He began tentatively. He had not intended to go down this path with her, but he owed it to Mick to try. Tilda followed his gaze. Her green eyes flared momentarily, and Jack could have sworn she was about to tear into him with one of those tongue lashings he remembered from his childhood. Then she gave a wan smile, her shoulders slumping again. She sighed, her breath carrying the scent of stale alcohol. Her eyes were misting up. She brushed a strand of her red hair from her face with a hand that had a slight tremor to it.

"I know Jack. Thank you for caring. This time of year… it isn't good for me. I feel particularly alone…I'll start looking for help. I don't want to make excuses, but when Jerry left, I didn't have time for counselling or grief stuff. I focused on work. Self-medicated."

She looked meaningfully at the bottle.

"Mrs O'Hare…" Jack began haltingly, "I don't usually get into this deep stuff…I mean…it's not over for you. You're not even fifty yet…are you?" Jack frowned, trying to do the maths, but gave up. "You can meet someone else. I mean no offence, but you're still pretty fit…if you gave yourself a chance…quit…"

He waved his hand at the bottle, and Tilda smiled. Jack suddenly realised how dazzling that smile could be behind those tired eyes.

"Thank you, Jack. People say yer an idiot, but at least yer an idiot with heart."

Jack half-smiled but with a deepening frown, not entirely sure if he had been insulted or complimented. Shaking his head, he reached into his pocket and pulled out his phone. He unlocked it, dialled Mick's number, and handed it to Tilda.

30/07/2020.

0730

Somewhere north of the Victorian Border.

They had been on the road for hours now. The road stretched off to the horizon, brightening in the light of the dawn sun. Thorne shifted in his seat. Hobson looked sideways at him. He was starting to become more than a little rattled.

"What!"

Thorne looked at her and cleared his throat.

"Where is he? We should've caught up with him by now."

Yet here they were, racing at one hundred and forty kilometres an hour and nothing.

"I know," muttered Hobson. She looked into the rear-view mirror. The hypnotic purr of the engine and the car's gentle rocking had affected Akina in the back seat. She sat slumped against the door. Fast asleep. Hobson turned her attention back to the road ahead as if *the Mutant* would come into view any moment. But nothing. Thorne had tried small talk with her several times, but she had answered with grunts. He figured he had nothing to lose.

"How far ahead do you think he got?"

"Can't have gotten *this* far. He's dodged us somehow."

"How? Who *is* this kid?" Thorne ventured.

Hobson looked at him. Weighing him. For a long moment, he thought she would return to staring at the road. She turned to look directly at Akina, who was still asleep.

"Michael O'Hare. He is the son of my ex-sergeant. Essentially, he's a good kid. His Dad was a very good man. Good sergeant. He stood by me. When I was younger, I was headed down a bad track. My parents didn't want a bar of their "dyke daughter", and at the time, the town was not exactly…open-minded back then. But he helped me one night. Before taking me home, Jerry sat with me, and we talked. He made me realise I was worth more than I thought. It's amazing when that kind of bond forms between people. He's why I joined the job. He stood by me against the hazing I copped in the 'man's world'. Convinced the machos to at least let me prove myself," A proud grin flashed across her face. "Which I did. Then, two years ago…" her voice cracked, and she gazed out of the window.

"What happened?" prompted Thorne.

Hobson cleared her throat.

"Nothing I couldn't have stopped if I'd been more switched on. A little less self-centred. Anyway. He looked out for me, so I owe him. Which is why I am trying to get his kid back with minimum fuss."

"Minimum fuss? You call this minimum fuss?"

"This is not how I thought it would go. I thought I'd be able to catch up with him and get him back to his mother without making it too official. I didn't expect to find myself crossing jurisdictions."

"You mean you don't plan to arrest him?"

Thorne was incredulous.

"No."

"Are you nuts? We are done if we don't arrest him after we catch him. After all this fuss, we can't go back empty-handed. Do you know how many calls I've ignored from my Sergeant? I'm screwed if I don't make an arrest."

"He's a good kid," said Hobson. "He just needs firm guidance."

Thorne started to slow the car down.

"What are you doing?" Hobson said. Her tone was almost bored.

"Turning around. Fuck if I'd known that was your plan, I would not have come."

"Listen, kid. Turn this car around, and you will be very sorry."

"Why? What are you going to do?"

"Nothing," said Hobson.

"Nothing?"

"Nothing."

The car stopped on the side of the road, and Thorne looked at Hobson, his brow furrowed.

"I won't support your story about a pursuit. I won't back you up when your superiors want to know where you have been for the last…however many hours it's been. I might even suggest you wanted to force me on a 'date' in Sydney, and I could not escape."

Thorne gazed at Hobson, mouth working.

"You bitch," was all he could muster.

"Kid, this service is very closely knit. I am trying to protect the son of one of our own. Sure, we will get our asses kicked. But an ass-kicking from above is not as painful as being ostracised by our community because they think you're…corrupt."

Their eyes locked. Hobson's cool held Thorne's wide. He nodded in sudden understanding. He looked ahead, then back at Hobson. He looked ahead again. Jaw clenched, he began to accelerate.

"Thata boy," smiled Hobson, fighting a pang of guilt.

In the back seat, Akina slouched. Eyes closed. Ears open. Mind racing. She pulled out her phone, intending to call Mick. There was no signal. Cursing silently, she put the phone away.

Emerald Police Station.

It had been a quiet night. Not a lot had happened in Emerald. Some underwear had been stolen from washing lines, and a couple of fights had occurred. Hobson was bored. She yawned, leaning back on the chair. Her eyes closed.

"If the duty sarge catches you dozing, you'll be cleaning out the cells."

The familiar voice of Jerry O'Hare caused her to wake with a start. Her chair slammed to the floor, and she leapt to her feet, a grin cracking her face. Her brain felt like jelly.

"Jerry…" The glee she felt sank at the sight of the pale man before her. "Fuck me. I knew you were sick, but…"

The pale man smiled wryly, and his grey sunken cheeks and yellowing eyes gave him a ghostly look. Hobson stared, a knot forming in her stomach as she saw within those eyes that there was pain…and fear. Hobson felt suddenly very sick.

"Thanks, but I'll be back on the beat in a few weeks. Buzz me in, please. I have a meeting with the inspector."

For a moment, there was the familiar crack of authority that had Hobson hitting the access switch to unlock the door. He opened it, limped through it, and headed down the corridor.

"I won the state judo titles last week. They want me for the nationals," She wanted to say something to keep him there.

"That's awesome…I wish I had been…there."

He could only speak a few words between rattling breaths.

"Maybe the Nats?"

The man nodded. Hobson's jaw clenched. She felt the urge to cry. Something was very wrong here. Swallowing, she spoke, her voice thick, fighting back tears.

"What brings you in at 0612 in the morning?" she gazed at the clock.

"Like I said, I'm on the mend...I...need a firearm. I...thought I'd get some target...practice before I came back."

He finished the sentence in a rush. His body was racked with coughing. He wiped pink, frothy sputum from his lips with a stained handkerchief. He leaned against the door briefly, fighting for breath before straightening. Hobson looked at him, mind frozen by what she was seeing.

"Really? I mean, you look..." she could not finish the sentence. She still could not reconcile what she saw now with her memory of the strong man from three months before.

He grinned wryly.

"Thanks," he said.

They stared at each other awkwardly for a moment.

"I'll just go....sign out a firearm...for the range."

Hobson nodded.

"Goodbye, Melanie."

Jerry smiled before limping off towards the corridor leading to the gun safes. Something was not right. Hobson moved to follow when the front door crashed open, and a man with bruises on his face and a bloody nose burst through. He occupied Hobson's attention for several minutes, and when she turned from taking the man's details, Jerry had gone.

30/07/2020.

0730.

Somewhere north of the Victorian Border.

"So...do you follow the footy?"

They had been travelling in awkward silence for a couple of hours, and Thorne was starting to feel self-conscious. The question took Hobson by surprise, and the car swayed slightly.

"No."

"Cricket?"

"During COVID?"

"No, I mean normally. The ashes, do you follow the ashes?"

"No."

They drove a few more minutes before Thorne said:

"Netball?"
"Jesus! If you must know, I follow *and* practice Judo."

"Judo?"

"Yes."

Thornes's brow furrowed.

"That's like...wrestling?"

"The grappling parts, yes. I follow it on YouTube. They often show the world championships."

"Right. I've always found it a bit slow."

"Three-minute bouts? Slow? Whereas five men standing in the middle of a field for five days staring at two others on a bit of earth is so gripping."

Thorne glanced at Hobson.

"I was watching the cricket once. I dozed off. I slept for about four hours. When I woke up, nothing had changed."

"There's women's cricket, too."

"Well, you put it that way. I'm sold. It's the gender that makes it boring."

Thorne blushed and gazed out of the window. Hobson looked at him, her shoulders relaxed slightly, and she smiled at Thorne.

"Sorry. I didn't mean to be short. I've practised Judo for years. I got my second Dan grading a couple of years ago. I'll be going for my Third Dan soon. Do you play cricket?"

"Second Dan. Wow, so you're like an expert."

"Not quite expert, but I can hold my own."

"What got you into judo?"

"Hey, you never answered my question. Do you play cricket?"

"Not since school. The job takes up most of my time."

"Right?"

Hobson's smile turned into a grin.

"What I enjoy, though, is curling up on the couch and watching some quality sci-fi."

Thornes's eyebrows shot up

"Science fiction? You're a nerd?"

Hobson grinned.

"Guilty as charged. I go to conventions and play role-playing games. Read it. Listen to it."

Thorne looked at her again.

"You…er…do this alone?"

"Nope. I often curl up with Naomi and watch Star Trek, Babylon 5 or Doctor Who."

"O. I see."

Thorne seemed disappointed.

"Do you? My folks couldn't. Small town. Black girlfriend. They're not the proudest of parents."

"Tough break. What does she do?"

"Chopper Pilot. She used to fly for the US Army. She came out here on retirement. We met when we were conducting a search and rescue. We kinda hit it off. Met for drinks afterwards, and boom. Here we are two years later."

A small smile crawled across Thorn's face.

"What?"

"Cop, and ex-marine chopper pilot. You two are badass."

Hobson smiled.

"You have a significant other in your life?"

Thorne shook his head.

"Nah. The job keeps me from meeting anyone."

"True that. But look, kid, don't let the job define who you are. Make sure you keep time for yourself."

A quiet voice floated from the back seat.

"I'm sorry."

"What was that twinkles?" Hobson snapped, her face hardening once more.

"I'm sorry. About your parents. It sucks when that sort of shit happens."

Hobson looked into the rearview, irritated at herself for forgetting Akina was there.

"Kid, if parents were one hundred per cent wonderful, none of us would leave home. But if we can get folks who at least show us they love us, well, that's a plus, I guess."

Akina sank back into her seat in deep thought.

The phone rang, waking Mick with a start. Looking at the dashboard clock, he saw that he had been asleep for nearly half an hour. He had pulled over to rest when he had yawned. He rubbed grit from his eyes and closed them for a second. To rest them. He had jerked awake just in time to stop himself from driving off the road. He had entertained drinking an energy drink and carrying on, but decided sleep was wiser and parked up. Setting his timer, he drank the energy drink before falling asleep. He figured the drink would already be in his system when he awoke. He yawned again and looked at his phone. Jack was calling. With raised eyebrows, he answered the phone.

"Hey fuck nuts," he said.

His mother's voice cut through the speaker.

"You mind yer language, Michael O'Hare."

Mick sat bolt upright and looked again at the name on the phone, wondering if he had been mistaken. Nope. Definitely Jack's phone.

"What's going on? Are you okay? What are you doing with Jack's phone?"

"Listen, young man," Her voice was a little husky, slurred. Mick bristled. The Irish accent floated out of the tiny speaker of the hands-free. "I'm fine. Jack is here because you sent him here, and if you don't remember, you should stop driving. Now! Mick. Jack's told me what's going on. Look, Mick. Things have not been great here, I know-".

"Have you been drinking?"

The question came out. Unbidden. His tone was sharp. In the pause that followed, Mick wished he could take it back. His accusing tone was not lost on Tilda.

"Look, I know what you must be thinking right now-"

"No! You don't. If you did, you would not have asked Jack to call."

As he spoke, Mick wondered why he could not shut up. This was not what he wanted to say, not the apology he needed to offer. His mind screamed, 'Shut up,' as he continued.

"Have you been drinking?" his tone was sharper than intended.

"Listen, Mick," Tilda's voice was pleading now. "I'm going to get help. I'm going to call the employee assistance program. It's offered at work-"

"Yeah, like you always say when you're drunk."

He said, cutting the connection. He glared bitterly at his reflection in the windscreen, his mouth twisting bitterly as he glared at himself.

"What are you doin' fuckwit?" he snapped to his pale reflection. "How'd that help? She rang to talk, and you treat her like that. He looked at the clock, and he found solace in anger. So she came home and tried to call him. She had a drink and slept.

"I bet if Jack hadn't turned up, she'd 've just gone to work," He snapped to his reflection. "Not missed me 'til she needed some groceries or something."

At least, though, he knew where he stood in his mother's list of priorities. The job. The bottle. Him. He started *the Mutant* and pulled onto the road. He was unsure whether it was his anger or the energy drink, but he was suddenly alert. The job. With a jolt, Mick realised the time. His mother should already *be* at work. Why was she not at work? Jaw clenched, Mick decided he did not want to think about it.

Tilda looked at Jack as the phone went dead. She handed it back.

"I think you had better be getting home, Jack. I appreciate your concern."

Her voice was suddenly cold, and her eyes were pained. Jack stood and, with a little relief, headed for the front door. He turned to look at Tilda.

"Is he okay?"

"As well as can be expected."

"Will you be okay?"

Tilda nodded with a wan smile. He nodded, closing the door on the way out.

With that, Tilda stood and headed to the kitchen to retrieve a bottle of wine from the fridge.

Hobson and Thorne climbed back into the car. She looked across at Thorne as he settled into the driver's seat, shoulders slumped, face pale.

"He must look how I feel," She thought, her jaw cracking as she yawned.

"Look, Thorne, I'm sorry-"

His red-eyed glare cut her off. They had been held up for an hour on the Victorian border. The New South Wales Inspector in Charge of this checkpoint had reprimanded them for crossing hard borders and ignoring jurisdictional boundaries. Complaints had been laid, and orders to return to Queensland and stand down, effective immediately, had been issued. They sat for a moment, staring across the Murray into Victoria, hopes of a career seeping away with the water as it flowed lazily past.

"How'd we miss him?" Snapped Thorne, slapping the steering wheel. The suddenness of his voice made Hobson jump.

Hobson shook her head, rubbing her grainy eyes.

"You're idiots, is how," chimed Akina.

"Shut it, Twinkles," snapped Hobson.

"Look. This adventure has been fun, but going by the missed calls on my phone, my inspector wants to speak to me," said

Thorne. "I...we are well and truly screwed. I should've never let you pull me into this without my sergeant's permission."

Hobson opened her mouth and clamped it shut. Thorne was right. She had jeopardised her future and his, which was unforgivable.

"Sorry," She said again. It was all she could think to say, but she meant it. Thorne looked at her. He looked like he wanted to say something else.

"What?"

"Nothing," said Thorne.

He started the motor and turned the police car around.

"Let's find a motel or something. Get some rest and then head back."

Hobson nodded. She hated to admit it, but she had lost. Mick had somehow evaded her. How or when, she could not say. Now, she had to accept the idea of apprehending someone at night in the middle of nowhere, which was ambitious. Hobson gazed out of the window, her eyes getting heavy. She cracked a yawn. It occurred to her that she had not slept for over twenty-four hours.

"Sorry, Jerry, " she whispered as they pulled around and headed back the way they came. Rounding a bend, Thorne suddenly yelled. Hobson sat bolt upright in time to see *the Mutant* heading towards them.

"Fuck," cried Mick, accelerating. He looked into the rear-view mirror as the Queensland police car conducted a perfect hand brake turn and accelerated after him. He had been ready to cross the border this time. Mick knew there was no way he would get across the border at the main crossing, so he had studied the maps on his phone and found a possible, if risky, alternative. But now, as he looked at the police car closing behind him. Lights flashing. He wondered if he would make it to the border. His phone rang. He looked at the caller ID. It was Hobson. Without thinking, he answered it.

"What?"

"Give up, Mick. You know how this will end. That thing can't outpace a Highway Patrol Vehicle."

In the background, Mich could hear another voice, calling for assistance over the radio.

"-we are…er…somewhere north-Hobson, what's the Sat Nav give out position as?"

Mick smiled. He could still use the confusion, but had to keep Hobson talking.

Putting his foot down, he sped up the road.

"Mel, what is your problem? Why can't you leave me alone?"

There was a moment's pause, and Mick checked that the line was connected.

"You said once I was not your Dad. Of course, I'm not, but over the years, I began to think of you as a little brother and Jerry as my father. The day he shot himself, I spoke to him. I let him into the police station. I should've twigged that there was a problem; my gut told me something was amiss, but I was tired and distracted. I feel I owe him. Owe you."

Mick slowed, taking a right turn a little too fast; *the Mutant* leaned its tyres, squealing. He accelerated up the side road.

"You owe us nothing. *You* didn't give him the gun. *You* didn't make him put it next to his head."

"Mick, you once said he was a coward, that he abandoned you and your Mum. He wasn't. The pain he was in. Wasting away. The indignity he had coming. He wanted you to remember him as a strong-"

"He didn't care about us," Mick cut across.

"His last thoughts must have been about you."

"How could you know that!"

"Look where he spent his final moment. Where you both used to camp, in the Fairburn, near Maraboon?"

Mick felt like he had been punched in the chest. The road ahead blurred. Knuckling tears out of his eyes, he slowed as he neared the end of the road.

"Fuck you," He yelled. His voice was thick, and he cut the call. He engaged four-wheel drive, his motor's tone dropping in pitch. He moved the 4x4 carefully up the embankment. The Highway patrol car was nearly up to him as *the Mutant's* motor laboured the embankment and pulled onto railway tracks. He headed to the railway bridge crossing the Murray.

"Dammit. I thought I had him," Hobson yelled, punching the roof of the car. Thorne gunned the police car after *the Mutant.* He knew that Mick now had the advantage; the low-slung vehicle was not designed for off-road travel. He glared down at the GPS mounted on the dashboard.

"That's his plan," He grinned suddenly as the car fishtailed after *the Mutant.*

"What is?" asked Hobson, bringing herself back to the here and now with some effort. Now wide awake, she clutched the side of the car. "Slow down, kid. You're not exactly controlling this car."

"There's a rail crossing upriver from the main border. He's aiming for that."

"We have him, then; there's no need to kill us. *The Mutant* is not a rocket truck, you know. Slow down."

Hobson looked back at Akina, now wide awake. She was bouncing around in the back seat of the car. She called out.

"Ease up, will you? I'm not a pinball."

"Can it, Twinkles, try buckling up. Damn it, Thorne, I said dial it back. He can't outrun us. We have him," Yelled Hobson from between clenched teeth as she hung onto the handle next to the seat.

This was too much for Akina.

"Dammit, Hobson, what is your problem? Why do you have it in for Mick?"

"Have it in for him?"

Hobson turned to look at Akina. "I saw you at the servo on Wednesday. I saved the CCTV. I'm going to put in a complaint to Ethical Standards."

"I don't have anything in for him. I am trying to help him. Help both of you. At first, I didn't know why he rabbited out of town. But when I realised you were together, I figured it out. "Why the fuck would you elope to Victoria, of all places? More freedom? That's a laugh. But-"

"Elope? What? No, you've got it messed up. We *are* together...I think...but we just got together. Last night. But this is about Con."

"Who?"

"Con. An old man that Mick is friends with on Grouplink. He's alone and going to kill himself today if we can't get to him by midday."

Thorne grunted as the car bounced off the road and up an embankment.

"C'mon, you stupid bitch of a thing," He screamed at the car as it slowed, wheels spinning as it edged slowly up the embankment.

"I don't follow?"

"He's an old man on Grouplink. Mick has been friends with him for a couple of years, since just after Jerry's death. He's been mentoring Mick with building *the Mutant.* I think Mick views him as a replacement for Jerry. Well, Mick thinks Con is going to kill himself. Not sure why. It has something to do with being alone in the lockdowns. Mick is trying to stop him."

Everything dropped into place. This made more sense than Mick eloping. A surrogate father? He is going to kill himself. And here she was, trying to stop him. The car lurched as it finally reached the top of the embankment. Hobson was thrown against the door as he swung the car with teeth-chattering bumps onto the track.

"Ha, there he is. On the rail bridge, I knew it. We have him. What's the Victorian State Police frequency?"

Mick smiled grimly as he pulled off the bridge. He looked into his rear-view mirror. He saw the police car pull onto the rail track and begin to accelerate. Looking around, he saw an off-road track leading off to the right. He grinned, thinking, "Low-slung cop cars aren't designed for off-road."

Thorne repeatedly glanced at the radio, his hand flicking between its dials and the steering wheel. The shaking of the car made it difficult to manipulate the fine dials. Next to him, Hobson looked at *the Mutant* edging off the rail bridge, down the embankment onto a rough-looking track. She looked again at Thorne, eyes wide, and aimed the Police cruiser at the entry to the bridge. For a moment, her mind locked. She could hear the motor and the clatter of rocks as they sprayed underneath the car. She looked again at *the Mutant,* and her jaw set. Thorne's voice echoed through the lock.

"Got it. Victoria border control. This is Queensland State Police constable Allan Thorne, 256. With a priority call, are you receiving it over?"

The puzzled reply.

"Victoria control receiving," The female voice at the other end sounded puzzled.

"Victoria control-"

Hobson grabbed the wheel, yanking it towards her. She had intended to run the car off the tracks and down the embankment below, but she miscalculated Thornes' panicked reaction.

Mick stared as the police car suddenly swerved, launching into the Murray. With an explosion of brown water, it came to rest. Bobbing, it began to rotate and float slowly downstream. Steam poured from under the bonnet. He slammed his brakes on and got out of the car. He ran towards the river, staring as the police car's nose dipped below the water. Then he grinned with relief as Hobson and the other cop pulled themselves out of the windows. Satisfied that they were okay and reassuring himself that Akina would be fine, Mick turned and ran back to *the Mutant.* He climbed back in, put *the Mutant* back into gear and headed off the rails towards the Goulburn Valley Highway.

"What the fuck you dumb-" the rest of Thorne's sentence had been drowned by the noise of the car impacting the water.

"We'd better get out. That goes for you, too, sweetie," Said Hobson over her shoulder. Hobson pulled herself out of the car's open window. Water began to flow in as she pushed her way clear of the vehicle. Thorne was doing the same on the driver's side. They swam back to the bank of the river and pulled themselves out of the water.

"You're gone, you crazy bitch. YOU ARE FUCKING GONE," He gasped, rolling onto his back on the embankment.

Hobson nodded, looking at the car. Its boot tipped up and slid under the surface in a cloud of smoke and steam. Hobson frowned.

"Where's the girl?"

Thorne shook his head.

"The girl?"

They looked over at the boot as it disappeared. Then it clicked.

"The child locks dip shit," cried Hobson; leaping to her feet, she ripped off her sunglasses and mask and dove into the water, striking towards where the car was disappearing.

"You're nuts. You'll get sucked under," Cried Thorne. He jumped to his feet and ran towards the nearby road to get help.

Akina lurched forward as the car hit the water. The collision with the partition between the back seat and front stunned her for several moments. Through the haze, she saw the two police officers unclipping their seat belts and pulling themselves through their windows. She fell against the plastic barrier as the car tipped. She anxiously reached for the door handle. Nothing happened. She tried again, anxiety turning to panic. The door would not open. She tried the window switches. They wouldn't lower. The car began to darken as it sank under the muddy waters. She felt her feet get wet as the river flowed into the car. Akina began kicking at the window in panic. The car started to fill more quickly as it sank. Tears flowing, she began screaming as the Murray flowed past her stomach and over her chest. She held her breath as it covered her head. She bashed at the window again with no effect. Her head began to spin. Her lungs began to burn. She felt her heart smashing against her chest. When she could no longer hold her breath, water flooded her lungs. Her world went dark, and her last thought was about how her parents would feel when they learned about her death.

By the time Hobson got to the car, it was deep. She swam down and grabbed the light bar on the vehicle's roof. Using that to pull herself in close, she could see Akina hammering on the opposite door. Hobson reached for the door handle. Pulled. It didn't budge. She stared desperately at the wide-eyed girl in the car. The muddy water enveloped her as she thrashed at the window. Kicking away from the car, Hobson moved to the back window, her lungs beginning to burn. She pulled out her baton. With the titanium end, it began to hammer at the window. A sudden flurry of bubbles inside the car puzzled her for a second before she realised it was Akina's lungs failing. Adrenaline coursed. Gathering her strength, Hobson bore down a mighty blow against the window. It caved under the baton. Her ears were ringing, and Hobson felt her lungs were about to fail. She pulled herself into the car, groping in the semi-darkness. Her fingers brushed cloth. Her hand hooked around a belt, and she struck desperately for the surface. With an explosion of breath, she burst into sunlight. Gasping for breath, she struck for the nearest bank. After what felt like hours, she hauled the limp form of the girl onto the rocky bank. Hobson took a moment, sucking in the air with massive breaths. The tingling in her fingers eased. When her head stopped spinning, she turned. Seeing the limp, unmoving form spurred her into action. Scrambling to her knees, she placed her hands on the girl's chest and began to pump.

Twenty minutes down the road, Mick pulled into another service station. His mind was racing. Guilt. Panic. Should he have stopped to help Hobson? Was Akina okay? Akina. Now that he had time to think, he could not remember seeing

Akina surface. Just Hobson and her plus one. He pulled out his phone and tried to call her again. However, her phone went to voicemail. Catching the clerk's eye through the service shop window, he hurriedly put the phone away and unhooked the bowser pump. He was terrified for Akina. What if she had been lost in the car when it went under? Why had he not stopped? He should have stopped. He considered giving up. Going back. Would Con have wanted all this trouble? What would be the final cost of this road trip? What had he lost? Why didn't he stop? He was barely able to keep his eyes open, and every time he rubbed them, they felt gritty. Why hadn't he stopped? Why *didn't* he go back? He felt like throwing up. Akina. He remembered a trick she had shown him once. Something to handle frustration. He took a deep breath, held it for two seconds, and then breathed out slowly. Mick closed his eyes, repeating it four more times. To his surprise, his mind began to settle. Things became clear. Akina was not answering her phone because the river water had ruined it. If he went back now, he could not help. If he quit, then all of this would have been for nothing. Sacrifices made for nothing. He *had* to continue, or Akina would slap him to next week the next time he saw her. He stood at the bowser filling *the Mutant.* He tried to distract himself by looking around. Looking for something, anything to stop himself from crying. His eyes landed as they always did on the four-wheel drives in the concourse. One was a nice but reasonably generic blue Triton parked in the bay next to the shop. It had a bull bar and nice lights, colour-coded. Two aerials, one standard CB, the other marine. In any other company, Mick might have been impressed. But the vehicle that caught his eye was a 1979 series Land Cruiser. He had to admit he had never seen anything like it. It was charcoal grey and shone. It had on top what looked like a barbecue, but the radiation warning decals on its side suggested otherwise. As his eyes followed its line, he took in its bull bar with its array of ariels, winch, and assortment of lights along its roof rack. His eye rested on the owner. He was a tall, heavyset man with a goatee. He wore a black bandana, black sunglasses, and a black mask with a skull jaw pattern on it. He was looking directly at Mick. A sense of unease overcame his grief. Mick felt he was being weighed and measured under that unflinching gaze. A female voice yelled from the cab.

"Ghost."

"Yes?" his voice was gravely. His eyes never left Mick.

"Just got a message. We need to get back to Bendigo."

"Roger that."

The pump in the man's hand kicked, and he turned, putting it back in its cradle. He headed over to pay. Mick looked into the cab's open window, and he saw a younger blonde woman studying a wad of papers. His pump kicked, signalling his car was full. He walked towards the shop. Ghost was in the shop speaking with two others near the coffee machine. They nodded, and the three of them headed out. Two into the Triton, and Ghost to his 79. Mick looked down, determined not to make eye contact with any of them. He walked over to the desk.

"G'day," He smiled at the clerk behind the counter. The man, an Indian, smiled politely.

"Good morning. Just the fuel?"

"Yes please."

The sound of two engines started up outside: the deep, throaty roar of the '79's 8-cylinder and the slightly quieter rumble of the Triton's diesel. Mick chanced a side-long glance at them as they pulled out and noted, with some relief, that they were headed in the opposite direction to him. He watched as a sizeable, half-loaded vehicle transporter pulled into the service station. The driver climbed down from the cab, looking with interest at *the Mutant*.

"Queensland plates," Mick thought, glancing at the front of the transporter. Then it struck him. His plates were Queensland. How could he have made such a dumb oversight? In the country on nearly empty roads, they didn't matter. But once he hit the outskirts of Melbourne. The cashier was speaking again, pulling him back into the here and now.

"What?" asked Mick, resolving to sort the plates issue once he found a parked Victorian car.

"I asked if I could interest you in two chocolate bars for $5?"

"No thanks. Just the fuel."

Mick paid for the fuel and headed out into the forecourt. He gave a weary smile at the truck driver, who grinned back. The driver called out as Mick was about to climb into *the Mutant*.

"O'Hare?"

Mick stopped and looked around uneasily.

"Whose askin'?"

"There's a roadblock up ahead waiting for you. About fifteen minutes up the road. At Numurkah."

"What?" asked Mick, alarm waking him up.

"A roadblock. I heard it on the scanner. Looking for your Ute. It's quite a good description, too. And names."

Hobson! Mick cursed.

"Cheers," He said. He reached for his phone to pull up maps.

"No probs, we Northerners gotta stick together."

Mick nodded. His mind was sluggishly trying to come up with an alternate route.

"Mate, you looked wrecked," The truck driver observed. He held out his hand. "My name's Terrence."

Mick looked up. He nodded absently and returned to his maps.

The man dropped his hand, looking at the boy with concern.

"What are you doing this trip for?" asked the man.

Mick looked at the tall man with a shaved head and goatee. He shrugged.

"A friend of mine will kill himself if I don't get to Frankston."

"True?"

The man looked at him appraisingly.

"True," Replied Mick.

"Maybe I can help you. Hang on a bit."

He finished filling his truck and headed inside.

Shivering, Hobson sat on the bank of the Murray, gazing at the slow-moving waters. She had a blanket wrapped around her slumped shoulders. There was a scream of sirens, and her head snapped around as the ambulance containing Akina pulled away. The paramedic, Jim, she thought his name was, the one who gave her the blanket, came and sat with her. He had a patch that read MICA on his shoulder. He smiled.

"How are you holding up?"

"Good. Thanks. How's the girl?"

"Touch and go. You did a good job with CPR; she was breathing with a rhythm by the time we arrived. We stabilised her and are taking her to Royal Melbourne's ICU. The choppers on it's way It'll RV with the road car in a field twenty minutes down the road."

Hobson nodded.

"It was a brave thing you did."

"Really? She would not have been there but for me."

"Still," Jim said. "You didn't have to go after her like you did. No one would have blamed you if you didn't."

"My sergeant taught me that the person you have to measure up to in this job is yourself. That way, if you fail, then you fail only you. I would have blamed myself for not going in there."

Jim nodded and decided to switch to a cheerful subject.

"Your mates okay too. I gave him the once-over. He'll be fine."

"My mate?"

Jim gestured to Thorne, who was speaking animatedly to Victorian Police on a radio borrowed from a local officer.

"Oh, him. He's not my mate."

"Oh. Right," Said Jim, sensing tension, changed the subject again.

"Will your sergeant mate be able to help you out of trouble here?"

Hobson did not look up.

"He died a few years ago."

"Right. Sorry."

Some days you should just shut up, he told himself.

"Well, good luck. You can keep the blanket."

"Thanks," Hobson gave a tired smile. She squinted in the morning sunlight. She wished she had her sunglasses. She looked around to see if she could find them. Footsteps crunched on the gravel. She looked up to see a New South Wales Inspector heading her way, her face like thunder as she glared at Hobson.

"Oh well. Time to face the music, I suppose," Murmured Hobson, climbing tiredly to her feet. She took one last glance at the direction *the Mutant* had taken, and with a wry smile murmured.

"Good luck, kid"

She turned and headed up the bank, ready to face the music.

They were on alert. There was a youth, Michael O'Hare, on the run from Queensland. He had evaded police through Queensland and New South Wales, causing the loss of at least two police vehicles, crossed two borders and was now loose in Victoria. This checkpoint was set up for O'Hare. The blue and white chopper circled the area, monitoring the off-road tracks. The BMWs of the Victorian Highway Patrol roamed the roads. Hunting. The police at the Nurmurkah block were determined to show Queensland and New South Wales forces how it was done. They were looking for a Ute. Four-wheel drive. It is unclear what the make is, but it is distinctive due to its olive drab paintwork. Rego MUT004. The police formed a line, waving down utes and pulling them into the checkpoints. Everything else, from motorbikes to cars to trucks, was waved through. The police officer looked up at the vehicle transport truck, taking it in with a bored glance. Shaking his head, the policeman waved the truck through, already looking at the next vehicle. The transporter as it rumbled slowly past, and the officer did not notice *the Mutant* loaded on the back.

"Ha!" laughed Terrence as they passed through. "Told ya."

Mick looked uneasily into the mirror at the police block, not sure if they could make him out through the windshield. They began to gain speed forward.

"Why didn't they stop you for a RAT test?" Mick asked, relief flooding through him as he began to feel the hours catching up to him. He yawned.

"They did that back at Tocumwal. They ain't interested in COVID. This is all for you. Better get in the back," Terrence gestured to the sleeping compartment behind him. Mick nodded. He slipped into the back and kept low. After a few moments, there was a quiet snore from the back. Terrence grinned. The kid needed sleep. Let him sleep.

"You can wake up now."

The voice cut across Mick's sleep, and a rough hand jolted him awake. He looked around, confused. Then he remembered. He was meant to be hiding, not sleeping.

"Sorry. I must have fallen asleep."

Mick realised the truck had stopped moving. Scrambling out of the sleeping compartment, he clambered into the cab. He tried not to look at the Playboy cutouts tacked to the walls; he did not want to consider what he had been lying in.

"No shit, you were snoring louder than my rig," Grinned Terrance.

"Are we past the block?"

"Mate. I got you to Melbourne. We're just outside Lilydale, about an hour or so from Franga. It depends on whether you follow the toll roads."

Mick was suddenly alert and unbelieving as he looked around at the green trees of Lilydale.

"What?"

"Us Maroons gotta stick together," Terrance reminded him. "Besides, the problems all this bullshit is causing us truckers. Mate, anything to stick it to 'em. I got your Ute down. Here's yer keys," He handed Mick the Keys to *the Mutant*. "Time for you to get yourself underway."

"What do I owe you?" asked Mick as he climbed from the cab.

"Nothin. Sometimes, it's enough just to help. Now get moving."

"I honestly don't know how to thank you."

"You just did. Go away now."

With that, the rotund trucker turned and headed back to his Mack. He heaved himself into the cab. The truck's motor turned, and the heavy vehicle transporter pulled ponderously onto the road. With a smile, Mick turned and headed to *the Mutant*.

"There are still good people in the world," He said to himself.

30/07/2021.

Frankston.

1300.

Despite the sleep in the truck, Mick had never felt as tired as he did when he finally turned into Lonicera Street. His burning eyes ached with the strain of staying open. His mouth gaped open with yet another yawn as he scanned the house numbers. He was confident that the Victorian authorities could learn a thing or two about road maintenance from Queensland as he bumped over yet another pothole. In the garden on the corner, he saw a small boy playing with cars. He looked up at Mick as he rumbled past and waved with a big grin, holding up a yellow and red roadster. Mick, despite himself, could not help smiling back, giving the kid a thumbs-up. He rolled along the road, cresting a hill, and began to roll down, seeing the street pull up into another hill. Number 26 sat in the dip; its burgundy wooden fence and white gates were tall but somehow welcoming. As he pulled up outside the house, Mick gave a tired smile. He had made it. He gazed at the house, his body aching, taking in the citrus trees along the edge of the drive, which led up to an old aluminium garage. Sighing, he sank back into his seat, suddenly unsure what to do next. He looked at the clock. 1303. He sat back up with a start.

"Dammit," He hissed.

Fatigue forgotten, he jumped out of *the Mutant* and ran to the gate. It was open a crack. Pushing his way through the gap, he ran up the drive. He bounded up the burgundy-painted steps to the screen door and reached for the doorbell when he noticed the door. It had been cracked open. His heart began to beat in his throat. Why would you leave it open? Mick tentatively pulled the door open and stepped into an entryway. It was small with windows, providing a greenhouse effect for plants on small shelves. He glanced at the collection of cacti and Venus flytraps before looking at the white-painted front door. It was wide open. He stood in a brightly lit hallway. The walls were cream and lined with photos. The house was silent. An odour, like a men's urinal, hung in the air. Not overpowering, but enough to make him wince.

"Hello?" he called out. The silence seemed to swallow his voice, which suddenly seemed harsh and abrasive to him. Mick stopped suddenly, his mind racing. What if he was wrong? What if Con had simply decided he had had enough of Grouplink? What if he walked in and found Con sitting on the couch watching TV with his wife? He might call the police, and then what? Mick yawned and rubbed his eyes. He shook his head to clear it. If he were right about what Con was like, then Con would be touched by the gesture and find the whole story hilarious. With his jaw clenched, Mick headed into the house. He found himself drawn to the photos on the walls. They were from other countries. Other times. But the same faces appeared in them, ageing as his eyes passed from one framed memory to the next. The carpeted floor creaked as he moved, transfixed by the photos that told the story of Con's life. Sepia photos of a Greek couple, conservatively dressed. She was in a black dress. He was in work clothes with a flat hat. Three children stood around them, grinning. Excited. The family stood at the base of a gangplank of a vast white ship. There were photos of the voyage and stops in different countries. There was a road trip from Sydney. The photos moved from the black and white sixties to the colours of the seventies. A wedding montage. Photos of Con by a large container ship. Family holidays in the 80s. A shot of the family in front of tall ships in Port Melbourne. High school valedictory photos. Graduation photos. More weddings. Grandchildren. So much joy. So much happiness. Mick stared at the wedding photos. Standing beside the bride, Mick recognised a younger Con than the one he knew from Grouplink, grinning. Mick's father would never be there for him at his wedding. A pang of jealousy stabbed his heart. It wasn't fair. Where were Con's children now? After he had been there through all those adventures and trials. Where were they when he needed them? He would never take his Dad for granted like that. His vision began to blur; rubbing his eyes, he was surprised to find his hands wet. Clearing his throat, he glanced at the rest of the photos. Grownups overseas. London. New York. Suddenly remembering where he was, he called out again.

"Con?" his voice cracked.

Turning back the way he came, he moved slowly along the hallway.

"Hello? Con?"

Steps muffled by the piled carpet, he moved back along the passage, drawn to two sliding doors at the end. To the left was an arch leading into a kitchen, and to his right was the front door. Escape. Ahead, two sliding doors. He took the handle to slide the door open and froze. His throat became dry. He began to hear his blood pumping through his ears. Why was there no answer? Was he too late? He looked around, suddenly feeling very lost. On his way here, in his mind, he was always going to make it on time. Just as Con finished his Grouplink chat, talk to him around. Now, suddenly, Mick was feeling very alone. He stood at the door, frozen. Not able to move. He suddenly felt very heavy. Not able to breathe. He stumbled back, leaning against the wall, and slid down, his face in his hands. He had an urge to run. Run out of the house. Get into his truck and head north without stopping. What if he opened the door and Con was dead? What would he do? Call the police? Tell them there was a dead man here? Face arrest here in Victoria? Maybe sneak away. Try to slip back into Queensland? What if he was wrong? What if Con was asleep? Thought he was trespassing? Had he called the police and was now hiding? He wondered where Hobson was now. Akina? Was she okay? He owed her so much. The thought of Akina galvanised him to move. Standing shakily, he moved back across the passage. He gripped the handles of the sliding doors and paused. And with a deep breath, he slid the door open. Mick looked into the bedroom. In the middle of the room was a large bed. In the bed lay a skeletal form. Unmoving, wrapped in stained sheets. The smell of stale urine and sweat was nearly overpowering. Mick wanted to vomit as he stared at the man in the bed. He felt like the silence was trying to crush him. His jaw slackened, and shaking, he dropped to his knees. His stomach churned, his exhausted mind struggling to accept what he was looking at. This was not how it was meant to go. The script in his mind said he would find a sad, lonely old man. A man so grateful for Mick's gesture that he would change his mind and choose life over death. From Grouplink and the photos he had just seen in the hall, he had expected to find an Adonis. A giant of a man. Jovial. Offering Ouzo. Food. A joke. Not this emaciated form. His knees were weak, so as he stood, he lurched to the side of the bed. He peered with exhausted fascination at the motionless face with pale, sunken cheeks. A tear rolled down Mick's cheek and dropped onto the old man's waxen face. Mick gave a startled cry as pale blue eyes embedded in yellowing sclera flared open. At the sight of Mick, they took on a momentary look of fear.

"Am I there? Is this heaven?" he asked in a hoarse, dry whisper.

"No," said Mick, his voice hoarse. He breathed heavily as he recovered from the shock.

"Then I am in Hell."

"Well," said Mick, "You're in Frankston, but..."

The older man's brow furrowed, and with a struggle, he sat up.

"I don't understand."

"I'm not sure I do either, Con, it's me. It's Mick."

This took a second.

"From Grouplink?" Wheezed Con.

Mick nodded. Con's gaze passed from Mick to a locked box on his bedside cabinet. Mick took it in for the first time. It was a lockable box, on which was a warning: *ingesting contents will cause death*. In front of the box was a wedding photo. A half smile cracked the old man's dry lips. He reached up and grabbed Mick's hand as if to reassure himself he was not hallucinating.

"Mick."

It was not a question. Mick nodded again, words failing him.

"But you are in Queensland."

Mick shook his head.

"Not at the moment."

"You broke lockdown. Why?"

"You seemed down. Like you needed…" Mick waved his hand at the box. "What's happening here, Con?"

Mick's voice was suddenly harsh. Angry. How could Con be so sick and not tell him? They were meant to be friends. Con flinched.

"Why did you come here? To be with an old, dying man? You were meant to be up to mischief."

"I don't know. I just felt you needed a friend."

Con grinned, showing nicotine-stained teeth.

"I do at that. But this was meant to be a private day. My day. Just for me."

Mick shook his head.

"What's happening here, Con? I don't get any of this."

Con broke into a fit of coughing.

"Water?" said Mick.

Con nodded, and Mick stumbled backwards, almost falling in his haste to leave the room. He headed to the kitchen, opened the fridge, and stood looking into it for a moment. Relieved to be out here, not wanting to go back. Not wanting to face the reality. Memories flooded in. His father had also started to lose weight toward the end. Is that how he would have ended up? He reached for a jug of chilled water. He filled a glass and took it back. He helped Con sit up, who then grabbed it and drank greedily. It was then that Mick saw, for the first time, how cracked the old man's lips were. Another fit of coughing racked his body. After his breathing settled, he looked at Mick.

"Con. Please. What is going on?"

Chest heaving as Con spoke, in his rasping voice, he said, "As a small boy in a country destroyed by war, when your parents tell you you're all leaving for a better life, it seems like a great idea. You leave the country and move to a peaceful one. You go to school. Get married, and everything is hokey dokey. But as you grow up, your parents… die. Brothers and sisters, they die, too. Your children grow up. Leave. Go and have their lives with their children. Far away lives, full of promise. You manage with your wife, and then suddenly, *she* dies. You look for someone and realise you are alone for the first time. Ever. You see, when you leave your country with your family at the start of your life, they don't talk about loneliness at the end. You share the excitement and adventure with people you love. But you must face death alone."

"What…?"

"Cancer. Lung. I have a few weeks at best."

Mick felt like he had been punched in the stomach. He looked at Con aghast.

"Don't make that face. I have had a good life. Look at the photos in the hall. But my wife. She died six months ago. I miss her. I don't want to spend the last couple of weeks of my life couped up alone, so…"

He waved at the locked box.

"What's that?"

"Medicine. It will end this."

"You mean…"

"They call it voluntary assisted dying. Don't be sorry for me, lad. I've had a good life, better than most. Five children. I've seen the world. I have photos in the hall…"

Con broke into a fit of coughing.

"Water," He gasped, grimacing with pain.

Mick turned, hurrying back out into the kitchen. When he returned, Con took the water with his emaciated but surprisingly strong hands. He sipped the water more slowly this time. When he spoke again, his voice was firmer. He gestured to the bed, inviting Mick to sit down.

"I saw the photos. Your life was amazing," said Mick.

"I married a beautiful woman. We met in the fields, you know. She was a wonderful person. She helped me join the merchant navy. She kept the house while I was out at sea. She raised the kiddies. When I had shore leave, she looked after me when I was fit and healthy. She cared for me here at the end. Until...she..."

"What happened?"

Con's crusted eyes misted.

"She fell in the backyard. She hit her head. I did not know she was out there. I had taken pain medication, see. I slept. I woke...I slept some more. I did not realise I'd slept a whole night. I thought it was the same day. That she was still at the shops. It was our neighbour who found her. She had fallen, carrying out the washing."

Tears ran down Con's cheeks. Mick, too, found tears running again.

"I'm sorry," He said, his voice as weak as the old man's. Somehow, it did not seem enough.

The old man grinned weakly. "Why? You did not push her. Stop wetting my sheets."

The right side of Mick's face twitched in an awkward half-smile.

"Where are your children?" Mick asked.

Con smiled proudly, his leathery skin wrinkling around his eyes.

"Dominic and Spiros are in Athens. Archaeologists are exploring our culture. They learn. And then teach. They are happy. Maria is a lawyer in New York. She is not married, but soon she will meet someone. I know it. Kristos is a literary agent in London. Married to a TV producer. They have three children, and George is mining in Western Australia."

"Surely you could get them here. To be with you?"

"No!" The man's voice suddenly became strong. "I will not have them pay $5000 each to sit for two weeks in a hotel room just to come and watch me die."

"So you want to die alone?"

"Yes. No fuss. No fanfare. Just peacefully on my own. But then you arrive, so I will not be alone after all. My only regret is that I'm not on my boat, the *Susana Marika*. I was in the merchant navy, you know. I spent most of my life near the sea. My father was a fisherman on Cos, in the boat his father built. Then the war came. Destroyed everything. Killed a generation so one man could feel important."

"Is that why your parents came to Australia?"

Con nodded.

"Yes. There was nothing in Greece. Europe was a mess. We came out in 1950. Fresh start. My father worked as a farmhand to pay for our school tuition. My mother worked as a housemaid in a hotel. Hard workers, to give us the start we needed in Australia."

"Do you have any brothers and sisters?" Mick's voice was a hoarse whisper now.

"They died."

Mick could have kicked himself for forgetting that Con mentioned this earlier.

"Have you *any* relatives in Victoria? Anyone I can call?"

Con shook his head.

"No."

He looked at Mick and reached out, patting the boy's hand.

"Hey, don't look so sad, my boy. I've known for a long time that I was going to die alone. I am ready for it. I look forward to the end of the pain. I was going to drink this today," He waved at the medicine. "Except I fell asleep. Again. I must stop napping."

"But you can't. You can't leave your kids like this," Mick burst out, suddenly angry with the old man.

Con was taken aback by Mick's sudden passion.

"Why not?"

"They deserve answers. Your kids. Your grandkids. They deserve to know you love them. Don't be selfish..."

Mick's tears of grief were now tears of anger. Con looked searchingly into Mick's distraught face, his expression suddenly very compassionate.

"I have spoken to them all over the last twenty-four hours. I said goodbye. They do not know what I plan, but they know I love them. And I have left notes for the grandkids."

Con looked at Mick, a small, sympathetic smile on his face. Mick suddenly realised Con felt sorry for him. *FOR HIM!* An old man in agony. Lying on his deathbed felt sorry for Mick. Mick felt suddenly ashamed.

"And you, young man. You drive from Queensland to stop a sad old man from killing himself. Why? What has happened to you?"

The room was silent, aside from the clock ticking, which Mick had not noticed until now. Mick started to speak but could not. He cleared his throat and tried again.

"My grandad was a miner in the seventies. Asbestos mines in Wittenoom. He met Nan and had a kid. My Dad. He spent the first ten years of his life playing in asbestos dust. They left when the mines were closed and moved to Emerald, where Dad grew up," Mick rubbed his tears away. "Dad became a cop. He was good. Fair. He'd try to help people rather than arrest them if he could. Three years ago, Dad was diagnosed with…It's incurable, see. Aggressive. He was in pain. He took his Ute out into the bush when they told him he could no longer work. No longer help people. He got his service gun, you see…he didn't even say goodbye. I didn't get a chance to stop him. He just up and…" Mick choked and then burst out. "So, you *can't* kill yourself. You can't. I'll call your kids. Tell them not to take you for granted."

Con smiled. "Oh, young man. I am so, so sorry. No boy should lose his father like that at such an early age. But you see, he wasn't being selfish. He wanted you to preserve your memory of him as a strong policeman. A protector. He did not want you to see him in that state. And you are not alone. You have your mother."

Mick knuckled his eyes. "But-"

Holding his hand up, Con continued, "It seems you have, unfortunately, focused on the wrong thing."

Mick gazed at the man through a hazy vision.

"What?"

"You are focused on what you lost. Grieving over what you never had. Bitter. You have missed what you still have. Your mother loves you, no doubt. And your memories of your father. Strong. Able. Not as..."

Again, Con waved his hand at himself.

Mick nodded, understanding dawning very slowly. He had been angry at Con's children for abandoning him. He had abandoned his mother.

"You have a young lady, I am sure?"

Mick nodded. "I do now...I think."

Mick's mind flashed suddenly to Akina, unmoving in a car full of water. 'Please not her as well.' He forced the image from his mind. Con was continuing to speak.

"And you have a job?"

Mick nodded.

"Your health? Your future? You have so much to live for. Why dwell in the past?"

Mick looked at the man. "My Mum does, she drinks. And works to forget. She should be over it by now."

Con shook his head.

"When a loved one dies, you are allowed to be angry. You are allowed to be sad. There is no rule about how long you must feel this way. It is different for all. Don't feel bad about feeling. Your mother? She is the same? She did not say goodbye to your father either. She would be preparing for it, but would not be ready. She, too, wishes she could have stopped him. She has carried guilt for what she has missed. She, too, was denied the chance to say goodbye."

Mick looked at Con. For some reason, he could feel the anger from the last two years eroding, ebbing away. He had not even considered this. Suddenly, the anger started to swell back. But this time, it was anger at himself. How could he have treated his mother like he had? What if, right now, she was depressed like he had thought Con was? Mick looked around helplessly. Con reached out a cold, dry hand and took Mick's.

"Young man. It is not too late. But the first person you need to forgive is yourself. You need to give yourself permission to forgive yourself for what you think you missed that day. You have no doubt struck out at those around you. Forgive yourself for that, too. You need to forgive your mother. Go back to Queensland. And let her know you are there for her."

"But-"

"Promise me," Con's voice was suddenly very firm. "She has suffered enough. All the more so because she has had to continue without time to grieve."

Mick looked at Con, then up to the window, and then back at the old man. Reluctantly, he nodded.

"That is a promise to a dying man. You cannot break it. Unfortunately, you have to deal with now. With your world the way it is. But this virus thing will pass. Things will return to normal. It can survive this if the world can rebound from the World Wars. Sure, you will have missed a few years. But you will still have so much to look forward to. I mean. In just 70 years, I have gone from living in a bombed-out hut in Cos to having grown children in Greece, America, and England. I have seen the introduction of the jet engine. Colour television. Video phone. Even in the 90s, if you rang overseas, you would get lag when talking to people. Nowadays, phew. Video link. Instant connection. No lag. I no longer have a phone on the wall, just this thing," He pointed to his mobile phone on the bedside. "And just when I thought society was soulless, dispassionate. A young man I barely know drives from Queensland, risking so much to save me from myself. Imagine what *you* will see. Mars colonised, perhaps. Self-driving cars. Maybe even world peace. Although compared to that last one, the Mars colony seems plausible."

Mick nodded. The last twenty-four hours were playing out in his memory: his fighting with his mother and Akina giving herself up so he could carry on. He had accused her of using the road trip as an excuse to run away. He now wondered if he was using Con as a means to run away. He suddenly felt tiny and selfish.

"But you can't go-" he began weakly. He felt he had to try once more, although he was starting to understand Con. Con gave an impatient snort.

"What do you want me to do? My wife? She is dead. The home support had to cut their visits because of the virus. Soon, I won't be able to make it to the bathroom. It is painful to breathe. My kids are weeks away, and even George is in

Perth. I will soon die anyway," Con lifted his chin, and his voice increased in volume. "Alone is bad enough. But I will not be found in a stinking puddle of my shit and piss. I will choose how I am found."

Con broke into a round of coughing; this time, flecks of pink foam formed at his lips. Mick hurriedly passed him a box of tissues and looked away as Con wiped his mouth. Once clean, Con took the wedding photo and looked at it. He hugged it and then put it back. They sat looking at each other for a long time, each lost in their thoughts. Mick broke the silence.

"Where is *Susana Marika?*"

"She is moored in the marina at Patterson Lakes. Twenty minutes away."

A slow smile crept across Mick's pale face.

"Does she have an autopilot?"

Con nodded, a look of hope in his eyes.

Mick grinned suddenly, wiping his eyes.

"You've never seen *the Mutant* up close. Fancy going for a trip?"

"You betcha. I bet my lights look better in real life," The old man grinned.

Mick stood up.

"You betcha. She's had a couple of dings on the way here but still runs a dream."

"One favour," Asked Con.

"Name it."

"Can you go to the front room? On the China cabinet, there is an urn with Marika's ashes. I was holding them so we could have a funeral with the kids. But that won't happen. I want to take Marika with me."

Mick stood up, stretching.

"What the hell. It's not like it can kill the mood."

"Good. Good," Smiled Con, "Now go to the bathroom. You will find a plastic chair with wheels."

Mick nodded, glad to be doing something. He stood and made his way down the passage to the bathroom. It was cramped, but the bathroom had a small plastic chair set on small casters. He rolled it awkwardly down the corridor back to the bedroom. Con tried to stand but needed help. Mick stared at the dark stain in the middle of the bed. Some of it was sweat, some of it other fluids.

"Carers to homes have been reduced. They are concerned about infecting me, making me worse," Spat Con.

Mick wheeled Con to the shower, hitting the walls several times with the unwieldy chair.

"I am amazed you got here in one piece," Con observed.

Mick helped Con undress. His jaw clenched as he helped wash away the dried, flaky residues around Con's body. He watched as the water pooled in the man's clavicle and ran through the channels made by the bones under the paper-thin skin. Mick knew the relief Con must have felt when he closed his eyes and turned his face into the warm stream. The old man smiled, revelling in the hot water, over his reddening skin, for what Mick suddenly realised was for the last time. Suddenly, Mick realised he did not know how the

Con must feel at that point. Mick suddenly felt sick; the heat of the shower was making him sweat. He began to feel lightheaded again as he gently washed away the grime. Con closed his eyes, turning his head up into the stream of water. Mick smiled. He could imagine how good that felt. Mick stepped back for a few moments. Exhausted. He let Con enjoy the sensation, of the water running over him.

"This is what Mum experiences every day," Mick thought, breathing heavily. "Except with what...four patients. No wonder she was so tired."

The shower took twenty minutes. With relief, he backed out, sweating and light-headed, from the humid shower. He helped Con dry off and shave. He watched as he brushed his thick, white hair. Within the hour, Con was dressed and helped by Mick down the steps of his house. He carried a shoulder bag containing the two medication bottles and the urn. The thick woollen sailor's jumper Con wore hung loosely on his thin frame. He had the blue denim peaked cap he wore as a merchant seaman jammed on his head. Leaning against Mick, he admired the final effect in the full-length mirror. He turned to Mick.

"Thank you."

Mick nodded.

"One last favour. Before we leave."

Mick looked at Con.

"My bed, can we put the sheets in the washing machine? I don't want my kids to see...that."

Mick looked at the stained mess and nodded.

Half an hour later, Con was smiling as he gave *the Mutant* parked on the curb a once-over.

"Given how you drive wheelchairs, I expected a parking style like this," Con said dryly.

"You could always walk," Mick laughed as he helped the old man up into the passenger's side and climbed into the driver's seat. He fired up the engine, noting fuel was low. He *had* to get long-range fuel tanks installed.

"We need to head that way."

Con gestured the way Mick had come. Mick turned *the Mutant* around and headed back up the hill. A police car crested the hill.

"Fuck," Hissed Mick.

"Drive casually. They will leave you alone."

"I think, Con," said Mick, looking into the rear-view mirror, "my Queensland number plates will suggest I'm out of my 5km zone."

"O dear, what an oversight," Murmured Con.

As they crested the hill, Mick saw the highway patrol's low-slung BMW turn into a driveway. The lights on the roof began to flash as the car backed out and pulled back the way from which it had come.

"Yup, they're comin' to say hi."

Con grinned regretfully as Mick pulled to the roadside.

"It was a nice effort. Thanks for trying, Mick. You are a good boy."

Mick smiled wanly as the car pulled up behind them.

"Tell that to my Mum."

A tall, broadly built policeman got out of the car. He put on his hat and adjusted his mask and eye shield as he approached the 4x4. The lights reflected off his high-vis jacket as he tapped on the window. Mick wound the window down.

"G'day," said Mick through the half-opened window, giving the police officer the grin he had copied from Jack.

"Good afternoon. Can I see your driver's licence, sir?" he asked as Mick wrestled with the window, which had jammed about two-thirds of the way down.

"Is there a problem, officer?"

Mick's tone was respectful.

"Where are you from?"

The question hung momentarily before Mick put his foot on the clutch and dropped *the Mutant* into gear.

"The great state of Gofukkit," He yelled as he took his foot off the clutch.

The V8 roared as *the Mutant* lurched forward, fishtailing as it thundered away. The officer looked stunned for a moment before turning to his car.

"What are you doing?" Cried Con, adrenaline giving his voice power.

"Helping you catch a boat," Said Mick.

Mirroring Mick's grin, Con gave a whoop and a laugh as *the Mutant* lurched off.

Behind them, they heard the siren start up. Mick's mind raced as he turned right. He knew the police car outperformed *the Mutant* in every way. He had to think.

"Sharp left down Monterey!" yelled Con.

Mick did as he was told. This was Con's town, and he knew his way through. He looked into the mirror and saw the police car streaking through the intersection. That would buy them a minute, he thought as he drove along the broad street.

"Where are we going?"

"I have an idea. We need a disguise."

"What do you mean?"

Mick wondered if the old man had finally lost it. In his rearview mirror, he saw the police swerve back into view.

"Take the next left onto Forrest Drive."

Mick did so as the police car gained on them. He shot along the narrower street, seeing the police car turn into Forrest and start to gain.

"Next left."

"Where're we headed?" said Mick through gritted teeth as he took the sharp turn past a school.

"Trust me."

As they sped along a meandering curve, Mick caught a glimpse of the police car turning into the street before disappearing behind the curve.

"Now, up here is a house with a load of old wrecks in the drive. You will have one try at this. There is a gap between the two Falcon wagons. Park between them. Kill the engine and get down."

As Con finished, Mick saw the house in question. The gap was thin. He aimed *the Mutant* at it. He crashed up onto the curb and slammed on the brakes. They slid between the two, the bumper stopping centimetres from the house. He killed the engine, and the pair of them ducked down as the police car flew past. They waited a moment before sitting up.

"See. Perfect disguise."

"But we are amongst wrecks," Said Mick, slightly hurt.

"Yes, and we fit in perfectly."

Smarting, Mick impulsively fired up the engine. Glancing into the rear-view mirror, about to reverse, he saw a rotund bearded man with a baseball bat blocking his way.

"Fuck," He cried, stalling the car with a lurch.

Con grinned, winding down his window.

"It's okay. He's a friend. Steve," He called breathlessly.

The man's furious glare softened.

"Con? Is that *you?* I was so sorry to hear about Marika."

"Yes. Thank you. How's your father?"

"Good. Mad but good."

There was an awkward moment.

"I need some help. Want to help me break the law?"

"What's one more?" Steve gave a toothy grin. "Who's your chauffeur?"

It was three in the afternoon, and it was starting to darken when they climbed into the Orange XY Falcon station wagon, which had been parked up the side drive. With Steve under the bonnet, it had taken twenty minutes to get it started. Sitting at the wheel, Mick gave the tarp-covered *Mutant* a regretful look as they waited for the police car to pass once again. When it did, they decided it was time to go.

"Remember," Steve called as they pulled out in a cloud of grey smoke. "Treat her gently, or you won't get there."

With a squeal of fan belts and a rhythmic tapping, Mick was sure it was not good. They moved steadily along the road. As they drove, Mick saw that the police car had turned onto the road and was heading towards them. This time, the heads of the officers were turned, looking into driveways. They passed each other. The police officers glanced at their car before carrying on with their search. The police car suddenly stopped, the driver's door opening. The police officer stepped out of his car and watched them. Mick stared intently at the rearview as the officer spoke into his shoulder mic.

"I know he said take it easy, but not this easy," Rasped Con.

Looking at his speedometer, Mick realised he had dropped to forty kilometres an hour.

"Do you reckon this car is registered?" Mick asked as they turned back onto the larger road from the side street.

"Knowing Steve, probably not. Why?"

"Me neither," Mick pushed the accelerator. The sluggish engine powered lethargically, and the car gradually gathered speed. They reached the end of the road and turned onto a service road bordering a main road. They drove half a kilometre before merging onto the main road.

"Patterson Lakes is back that way," said Con. "There's a break in the median strip in about two minutes, you can use for a U-turn."

Mick cut across the deserted road and bumped onto the median strip, to a surprised, "OOF! Or you can cut across the strip," from Con.

They headed in the opposite direction along the highway, past a sign reading 'Frankston Dandenong Road'. They took a left on a corner lined with closed shops. Looking in his rear-view mirror, Mick saw the highway patrol car burst from Forrest Drive and slide to a halt at the intersection. Mick willed the fifty-year-old wagon to stay in one piece as they bounced on, unsure if they had been seen as they swerved around the corner.

"How are things with your mother?" Said Con as they headed towards the freeway.

The question took Mick by surprise.

"Alright, I guess. Why?"

Con looked at him.

"Your comment earlier. 'Tell that to my mother. ' What did you mean by that?"

"What, you want to talk about this now?"

Con nodded. "It's not like the roads are so busy you need to concentrate."

Mick paused, gathering his thoughts. "When Dad died, Mum and me were close. We needed each other. She would come into my room. Climb into bed, cuddle up to me and cry herself to sleep."

Mick sat glaring out at the freeway.

"Go on," Prompted Con.

"Well, then Mum started drinking. Working all hours. We've been fighting a lot. I can't help it; she just makes me angry."

"Is it her you are angry at? Or are you just choosing to vent your anger about your father at her?"

"I'm not choosing anything. I didn't choose this life."

Con smiled at Mick.

"The thing is, we cannot always choose what happens to us. What we can choose is how we react to these things. You can choose to shout at your mother, or you can choose to leave the room and come back with a cooler head."

"But…she drinks."

"How much time each day do you spend working on your truck?"

Mick shrugged.

"Why do you do that? To distract yourself. From how you are feeling. Your mother is doing the same. She is numbing the pain."

"Does she hit you? Are you starving?"

"No."

"Throw things at you? Yell at you? Steel?"

"No."

Con smiled.

"People drink because something is missing in their lives. I don't know who else she has in her life right now, but what she needs from you is understanding and compassion, not judgment. She needs you to help her fill that void. She needs to know you love her. Unconditionally. Drinking or not."

Mick gazed at Con momentarily as the man echoed his earlier thoughts. He again felt tiny.

"I need to call Mum."

Con nodded.

Mick pulled his phone out and dialled his mother. The call went to the message bank, and with an exasperated tsk, he ended the call.

"Message bank," He explained to Con. Who just nodded and smiled.

Habib spoke again into his shoulder mic. "Peninsula control, this is 1988; we are pursuing a 1970 Ford Station Wagon, Orange, poor condition, index LET 818. Last seen in the area of Frankston Dandenong Road. There is a high probability that the occupants are from Queensland, possibly having travelled through New South Wales. Over?"

After a moment, a reply crackled over the radio: "Are you requesting air support?"

"Roger that. If available. Over?"

Habib gazed up and down the road. Forbes came to join him. He looked at Habib's face and knew to say nothing. Although Habib was new to the area, Forbes had realised quickly that he was good. A thinker. And when he was in deep thought, it was best not to interrupt him. Habib was gazing up and down the empty road. Where were they headed? Why here? He thought again about the occupants of the four-wheel drive vehicle. He was sure they were the same duo. The driver was average-looking, but the older man was dressed strangely. Thick navy-blue jumper, navy hat. Navy...that was it. He was dressed as a sailor. But why?

"Forbes. Is there a marina in Frankston?"

"What, for boats and shit?"

Habib looked across and nodded.

Forbes shook his head.

"No, the nearest is Patterson Lakes, about ten clicks down the Freeway."

Habib nodded. "Get in."

They sat gazing at the gate leading into the marina. It was solid enough to satisfy the marina's insurance policy. Mick reflected on what to do. He had not banked on the security guard flatly refusing entry.

"But I am a member, and this is my guest," Wheezed Con.

"That does not matter. The marina is closed to visitors. Leave, sir, or I *will* call the police," He'd said.

"What now?" asked Con, echoing his thoughts. In the distance, he heard a police siren.

Mick backed the wagon up as far as possible and put it back in park.

"Not sure. What do you want to do?" Mick looked at Con, who appeared to be in pain. "Perhaps you should drink some of that morphine."

"Not yet. Do you have a plan?"

"Besides trespass? No."

"Surely it would only be trespass if I weren't a member."

Mick nodded, wondering if that would hold up. He guessed a good lawyer would be able to help him with that. Come to think of it, Leanne's Dad was a good lawyer. He'd have to be, to be able to keep Jack on the streets. Mick considered all the charges stacked against him. He shrugged. What would one more be? They sat for a moment, the car ticking in neutral, before Mick said, "Your friend Steve, do you think he'd be angry if I dented his car?"

"Not much if it was for a good cause. But that's a substantial gate," Observed Con.

"This is a pre-90s car. *That's* solid."

With a sudden grin at Con, Mick dropped the wagon into gear. Holding his foot on the brake, he powered up and added, "Also, the mesh fence next to it is piss weak."

Con nodded, bracing against the seat and the door. Mick let the break go, and the car lurched forward. Mick winced as he crashed through the fence to the left of the gate. The guard raced out of the watch house. He headed down the road to the jetty as the guard pulled out his phone.

Mick watched as *Susan Marika* disappeared around the head towards Port Phillip Bay. Clutching the old denim hat Con had given him, he stood staring long after the boat had become a speck in the swell and then disappeared. Staring out to sea, he was lost in his thoughts. Deflated and exhausted. The wind had whipped up and was starting to drive rain. Still, he did not move. His thoughts were with his mother. She had been an only child. Born in Ireland, her parents now live in Tasmania. She had not seen them in over two years. She had lost track of her aunts and uncles at an early age. She, too, was alone in the world except for him. For her, he was everything. Was this the future she had resigned herself to? Dying alone? Had he fed that belief, pushing her to fill the emptiness in her life with work and, when not there, to numb the rest with wine? And her work. Massaging the small of his back, he thought about his experiences over the last couple of hours. He had never thought nursing was so hard. She would talk about being tired after helping out with washes because they were short on the floor, but until then, he had not realised what that meant. He needed to do better when he got back. Take her less for granted. Ensure she understood that she would never be alone. The sound of a helicopter above dragged him away from his thoughts. He looked up and saw the blue and white helicopter of the Victorian Police hovering above him before gliding off in the direction Con had taken. He'd only spent a short while with the man, yet in that short time, he had achieved more than his counsellor had in twenty-three sessions. He knew what he had to do. He just wished he had more time with Con while he did it. Taking a deep breath, he yelled out to sea.

"Be good. Or be good at it, Obi-Wan. Say hi to Marika for me. And thank *you*."

Turning, Mick needed a moment to take in the sight of the police BMW at the end of the pier. It was pulled up behind the old station wagon. The two officers waited, leaning against the wagon's dented bonnet. The taller of the two coolly beckoned him. Mick considered jumping off the jetty and swimming for it, but he did not want to abandon the wagon. Besides, by now, they knew who he was. They would get him eventually.

"Well, this seems a good time to start making better choices," he murmured. The police appeared in no hurry, so Mick reached into his pocket and pulled out his phone. He unlocked the screen and dialled his mother's number. The phone rang. It was weird, but he could not do this with the cops looking at him. He turned his back on them. The call went to the message bank. Of course, 1600. His mother would be on shift.

He began to speak. Choked. He cleared his throat. Tried again.

"Ma. I'm sorry. I was a dick. Dad's death wasn't your fault. I get it. I want you to know I won't leave you. I'm coming back. I *am* in a bit of shit, though. By the time you get this message, you will have discovered how much. I don't need your help, but I'll do my best after this. Love you, ma."

With a sigh, Mick wiped tears from his eyes. He tucked his phone into his pocket, turned, and headed back along the wharf.

Hobson looked sceptically at Jack, taking back the breathalyser, barely glancing at the 0.0 reading. He grinned back, meeting her eye as he gestured out of the driver's window at the front of the Patrol.

"Honestly. Last night. I must've hit something off-roading around Fairbairn. Don't unroadworthy her; I'm headed to the scrappers for a replacement now. Call 'em. Check if you want."

"What did you hit?"

"I don't know, Mel, it was dark. Wallaby maybe."

Hobson cast her eye over the rest of Jack's Patrol, taking in the gear on the roof rack.

"Off for a weekend camping?"

"That's not illegal again, is it?"

Hobson detected something in Jack's tone. Irritation? Anxiety? Her thoughts were interrupted by an irritated shout down the line.

"C'mon Hobson. Book him if he's over .05; otherwise, move him on. You're holding up traffic." Yelled Senior Constable McNair. Hobson looked along the line of traffic at the breathalyser station.

Looking right, she saw that Jack was the only driver in the queue. Looking left, she saw a tailback. She started to reply.

"Sorry, boss. Just pinging this man for-"

"I honestly don't care. You're not here for roadworthiness. Just get things moving. It's rush hour."

Hobson glared up the line at the police team leader, who was looking back at her. Then, she shrugged and waved Jack on.

Looks to be your lucky day. Don't think I won't be following this up. Make sure you get that light fixed."

"Thanks, Mel," Jack said behind his grin as he pulled away. The line of traffic began to flow out of the stop as the following line was brought in. This was the pattern for the next twenty minutes until she received a tap on the shoulder. She turned to find herself looking into MacNair's small, dark eyes, which glared up at her.

"You're being redeployed. Something to do with bikers in Fairbairn. They want you there. NOW."

Hobson's heart leapt at the break in the monotony. She nodded and headed towards where she had parked her car, weaving between the cars that had to be picked up by sober drivers. It wasn't that she could not see the value of these duties, but she was bored. She climbed behind the wheel of her Cruiser, eased it out and flicked on the lights and sirens as she headed out along the road towards Emerald.

The doorbell rang, and Mick focused on his gaming console, not hearing it through his headset. The vehicle he controlled crashed through a fence and cut across the country as he aimed it for the next checkpoint. There was a splintering crash, and the 4x4 bounced across the scrub. The doorbell rang again. Mick saw Tilda come from the kitchen in the corner of his eye, glaring irritably at him and hurrying to the front door. Aware that something was happening in the real world, Mick paused the game, dislodging his left earphones. He heard voices at the front door. His mother and...Mel. He grinned, standing up. He placed the controller on the table, interlocked his fingers behind his head and knelt on the front room floor. Hobson walked and stopped, looking down at him.

"That wasn't funny the first time, and it gets less every time you do it," She said.

Grinning, he stood, and they stepped forward and hugged each other.

"I don't have long, and I'm going to a job. I thought I'd swing past en route. First things first," she said, dropping to her knee and checking Mick's home detention ankle bracelet.

"Huh. All good. I cannot believe it's you and not Jack wearing this thing."

"I know right?" He paused. "Have you heard from Akina?"

"She's good. Came out of quarantine this morning. She gets home in about an hour. Don't get your hopes up. Her Dad still wants to end you; she was in the ICU for a while, you know? She needs rehab."

Mick's face fell.

"I know."

Hobson paused, remembering those tense moments she dragged Akina's lifeless body onto the shore of the Murray. Pumping her chest. It had been hit and miss, and Mr Sato was not wrong to be angry at Mick. But things were starting to turn out okay.

"Look. I put in a word for you again. Explained to him, again, that it was Akina's choice. That you and Akina have strong feelings for each other. Trying to come between you will push Akina away. He seemed less homicidal toward you today."

"How does he not blame you? It was your car…sort of."

"I'm a cop. He respects cops, plus I got the commendation for rescuing her."

"Any word on the disciplinary board?"

She tapped her shoulder.

"Can't you tell? I'm back to a constable. Tied to a desk or sent on the shittiest assignments. Like this one."

She gestured to Mick's ankle.

"Sorry."

"Don't be. I chose to come after you. I knew what I should've done. To be honest, I'm surprised I'm still in the job. That one's down to Leanne's Dad. He's pissed me off in the past when he's gotten perps off, but given that, I should've been sacked. Thorne, too, though he's back to general duties. Still, to 'help keep me out of trouble', the Super has me going on course after course. The latest is 'profiling the criminal from the scene.' It does me no good when I'm behind a desk, but at least I am learning. Any word on *the Mutant*?"

"Yeah. I found the guy who has her. He's agreed to send her back up once I can get the money for the transport."

"I can-"

"No," Mick cut in. "You've done enough. I need to do this one on my own."

Hobson nodded, smiling.

"Your father would be very proud of you right now."

Mick looked away.

"Thanks. But as proud of me as he might be, he'd be more thankful to you for how you've watched out for me. Sorry, I was such a dick."

"You were a grieving kid. Behaving as a grieving kid. I could have been a little less...severe, I suppose."

"Damn straight...still...it's weird to realise that you kinda stepped in there and were a sorta father...thing. Thanks."

Hobson looked through to the kitchen, where they could hear Tilda pottering.

"How is she?"

"Better, I think. She started day rehab with Salvo's last week. Her grief counsellor got her into it. There's a program for carers to help us understand addiction. I think I'll do it," he held up crossed fingers. "Let's hope."

"It'll be a long journey. But then you like long journeys...so..."

Hobson smiled. A nice smile, Mick realised.

"You should smile more often, Mel. It's nice."

Hobson blushed. For her part, Hobson had started grief counselling to help her work out her feelings about Jerry's death. It was helping.

"Anyway, gotta go. A kid found a body on the road out of town. I'm off to cordon off the area. Yay, it's the third one this week. We'll catch up."

"Third?"

"Yes. The first was a dog in a bag that had been beaten to death. The second was a bag of clothes that had fallen off the thrift shop truck. My hopes aren't high."

Mick nodded, understanding.

"Stay safe," he smiled as Hobson stood and left the room. A couple of moments later, the sound of the powerful V8 cut through the peace. Mick sat for a long time. Thinking. He had been honest. Once he looked at her attitude, he realised that all Hobson had tried to do was step up as a father figure. As a young teen, he had been too consumed with grief and anger to recognise it. As an older teen, I was too bitter to consider it. And then there was Con. Mick's jaw clenched as he considered the old man. He looked at the ragged denim hat which sat on the mantle. The Coast Guard had intercepted *the Marika* out at sea. Con was not on board. The police found the empty medicine bottles on board, rolling with the urn containing the ashes. The running theory was that he had fallen 'asleep' on deck, and the swell washed his body overboard. Mick considered something the man had said.

"You are focused on what you lost and what you never had. Not what you still have."

Walking over to the gaming console, he switched it off and then went to the kitchen. Tilda was standing at the sink, washing up the things from last night's dinner. She looked at him as he walked in. He could see a hint of excitement in her eyes, something he hadn't seen.

"Hey, Mum, how was your day?" Mick asked awkwardly. It was odd how often you started a conversation without saying anything.

Tilda took a deep breath, trying to steady her nerves. "Oh, it was quite interesting, actually. I, er, have a date tonight."

Mick raised an eyebrow, surprised. He felt a twisting in his guts but forced it down. This was good news.

"Really? That's great! Who's the lucky guy?"

"His name is Peter. He's a paramedic," Tilda replied, her voice shaky.

Mick chuckled.

"Peter the paramedic? That's a catchy name!"

Tilda managed a small laugh, feeling a bit more at ease.

"I suppose it is. He's really nice. We have lovely chats when our breaks allow. You'll like him; he likes four-wheel driving."

Mick's expression softened.

"I'm glad to hear that, Mum. You deserve someone nice. How did you meet him?"

"We met at the Urgent Care Centre. He was dropping off a patient, and we just started talking afterwards," Tilda explained, drying her hands on a towel.

"I'm happy for you, Mum. Where are you going?" Mick asked, genuinely interested.

"To that new Indian restaurant. I'm a bit nervous, to be honest," Tilda admitted, her worry returning.

"Don't be. Just be yourself. If he's as nice as you say, he'll appreciate you for who you are," Mick reassured her.

"Thanks, Mick. I was worried...well, I don't want you thinking I'm replacing your dad," Tilda said, her eyes glistening with gratitude.

"I know you're not, Ma. Just make sure to introduce me to Peter, the paramedic, soon. I need to see if he lives up to the name!"

Mick joked, giving her a playful nudge.

Tilda smiled, feeling a warmth in her heart. "I will, Mick. I promise."

Mick moved to the sink to help Tilda...help his mother with the dishes.

Hi there.

I hope you enjoyed the book. What follows is the first chapter of the next book of this series to give you an idea of what is to come.

Constable Melanie Hobson stood by the police tape, her keen eye scanning the bushland area around. She gave a bored sigh as the coroner lifted the tape behind her and moved past, walking unevenly across the forest floor. Hobson heard Harper Jones, the crime scene photographer, taking photographs of the scene. Hobson looked across and saw Jones had turned the camera from the body to an eucalypt.

"What ya got?" she called to the photographer, interest piqued.

"In that tangle of moss and twigs. A nesting pair of *Aprosmictus erythropterus*." Smiled Jones, a twinkle in her eye. Hobson gazed with casual interest high up in the trees. Sure enough, about seven meters up, she could make out the green head of a parrot popping out of the top of a pile of twigs.

"Red-winged parrot. Cute," she smiled.

"Very good, constable. I never knew you were a birder."

"Not obsessively. It's a casual thing. My counsellor got me into it. She used to say If you appreciated birds, you would never be bored," Hobson replied.

"This is true," Jones agreed, letting the camera fall against her chest, "When I watch them going about their business, it helps ground me. I realise that I'm okay as long as I have food and shelter."

Hobson nodded, smiling, "But then I see something like this."

She gestured to the body, doctor Coogan now kneeling next to it. Jones gazed solemnly at the man, nodding slowly. From her vantage point, Hobson looked at the body's orientation and then up to the nest in the tree. He had been facing the tree when he fell. Birdwatcher? With a groan, Coogan stood and made his ungainly way back.

"What do you make of that camera?" Hobson called.

The photographer glanced at the camera near the outstretched hand.

"Noice. Middle-range type with a 400mm lens. Great for nature photography, although not professional-grade. About six grands worth."

Hobson turned her attention to the large man pushing past her.

"What have you found, Doc?" she asked.

Coogan looked at her momentarily and, with a shake of his fleshy cheeks, which dislodged beads of sweat, said, "Male. Late twenties, shot twice from behind by two arrows. Broad heads. One through the right side of the chest and the other through the left. Good shot, I'd say, through the heart. Death was almost instantaneous, about twenty-four hours ago. Such a waste."

"From behind?"

Hobson looked around the forest. About thirty meters away, she saw a thick copse.

Coogan nodded.

"So, he fell forward?"

"Most likely. Well, I've got to head back out of this damned humidity. Tell the detectives if they get here, I'll have a report for them on their desks and not to harass me for it."

"You know, Doc, if you came with me to the gym, we could shift some of that weight and make life a little more comfortable for you."

Coogan stopped waddling and turned awkwardly, trying not to lose balance with his heavy medical bag.

"Are you a doctor constable?"

Hobson grinned playfully at the overweight man in front of her. She liked the irascible Coogan.

"No. But I have a level two first aid certificate, will that do?"

Coogan gave a rare smile.

"Perhaps you could order one online; everything else seems available online today."

"No, I thought I might get mine from a cereal packet. What brand do you eat?"

Coogan laughed, turned and shuffled away. Hobson noted that the man had not answered her question. She turned and looked at the body lying on the ground twenty meters away from the tape. Not far from the body, a camera lay smashed on the ground, its large lens broken away from the case. A backpack was leaning against a nearby tree, a steel drink bottle clipped onto the side. Her brow furrowed, she ducked under the tape and moved to the backpack. She knelt as she put on a pair of blue nitrile gloves and hefted the pack. It was heavy. She began to unzip the bag when a voice cut across the scene.

"Can I help you, *constable*?" There was an emphasis on the constable.

Hobson's shoulders slumped. She stood and turned to face Inspector Mancini.

"I was going to ask you the Alfrede question, *sir*."

The sir spat from under a curled lip as he glared at the skinny forty-something before her, the trusty sergeant Perkins to his right.

"Standing guard at the tape generally means being on this side. Lookin' away from the crime scene. Not, you know, poking around."

"Yeah, well, I thought you might need a little help. You seem lost when you need to think...sir," she smiled.

Mancini seethed.

"Stay in your lane, Hobson. Just because you're manning a crime scene doesn't mean you know how to handle a real investigation."

Hobson's face flushed with anger, glared at Inspector Fredrick Franco Mancini, who stood at the edge of the taped-off area, dabbing at the beads of sweat on his brow. He had made a big show of being in charge of a murder scene but refused to get his shiny shoes muddy. He stood, looking around. Chewing his nicotine gum, his chin moved furiously under the moustache, which started under his nose and worked its way down either side of his chin.

"Is that what you think? I've proven myself time and time again, and you know it."

Mancini sneered. "Proven yourself? A year ago, you pursued a perp, unofficially interstate, and crashed a police car into the Murray. All right, you saved, what's her name, from drowning? You're here because I let you stay, Hobson. If you're bored, then quit."

Hobson squared her shoulders, her eyes locked on Mancini's.

"I would not give you the satisfaction. Sir."

A tense silence hung in the air, broken only by the rustling of dry leaves in the breeze. Mancini shook his head, his frustration palpable. The sound of a motor approaching caused him to see a police land cruiser approaching the scene. Looking back at Hobson, he snarled, "You're on thin ice, Hobson. Stay out of my way, or I'll make sure you're stuck on booze buses forever."

The motor of the Land Cruiser cut and Mancini turned his attention fully in that direction; his chewing slowed as the passenger door opened. Hobson noted with interest the dark-skinned man who stepped down from the passenger side. He was dressed in a loose grey suit, and his greying hair framed a face obscured by large dark glasses. An old leather messenger bag hung over his shoulder and down to his right side. He looked around, taking in the scene. The stranger made Hobson think of a Bollywood hero. He walked up to Mancini, holding up his ID wallet for the inspector to see. Mancini smiled, showing yellowing teeth, as he greeted the senior officer. A homicide detective, Hobson guessed. They shook hands and spoke briefly before Mancini lifted the tape for the stranger to duck under. The stranger shook his head and went to the back of the car. Lifting the boot, he unshouldered his bag and placed it in the boot. He rummaged around the boot momentarily before pulling out two white packets. He handed one to Mancini before tearing open his own. It was a set of white coveralls, identical to those worn by Hobson. The detective gestured towards the body. As they approached the cordon, Hobson caught the end of the conversation as they reached the bottom, breathing heavily.

"…Hobson, who secured the crime scene."

The stranger nodded at Hobson.

"Also, sir, I notified the coroner. He is sending the local accredited undertaker to collect her."

"Good work, constable." The man looked around. "Do we know who he is?"

He spoke with an Indian accent. He smiled pleasantly at Hobson and gestured to the edge of the scene. Ignoring Mancini's smug grin, Hobson smiled and headed to the tape.

Hobson turned, "Not just yet, sir. I was just about to look through his belongings for ID when Inspector Mancini stopped me."

"I felt the forensic pathologist should-"

"Oh, he's been, sir. Dr Coogan was uncomfortable in the heat and said You'll have his report on your desk."

Mancini glared at Hobson, "Thank you for mentioning that constable."

"You're welcome, sir."

The stranger held his hand out to Hobson, "I am Detective Superintendent Drishti Ram, State Homicide Division."

Hobson took his hand, "Constable Melanie Hobson. Emerald Police."

"Pleased to make your acquaintance."

Ram smiled. "Doctor Coogan, you say? I know him. That man needs to eat less and move more. As a medical man, you'd think he'd know this."

Hobson nodded, returning the smile. "He said the man had been shot in the back sometime yesterday. Twice with a bow and arrow. Death was with the second shot."

The man nodded as he looked at the body. Hobson turned and began to walk away.

"Hunting accident, sir," Mancini said with finality.

"You think?"

"Yeah, it happens around here. Someone's hunting for Roos and sees a movement in the bush. This bloke dressed in camo gear and boom. Deader."

"Maybe."

Hobson snorted as she ducked under the tape.

"You have something to say, *constable*?" Mancini sneered.

Kicking herself, Hobson turned to the Inspector.

"Er, no. You are right. About hunting, but this was no accident."

"Really?" snapped Mancini as Ram said.

"Please go on, constable."

Awkwardly, Hobson looked at the two men and cleared her throat.

"*I* think this man was followed, no, stalked by a sadistic hunter. I think that the hunter saw his opportunity and took his shot. From over there."

She pointed to the copse thirty meters away.

"Bullshit." Spat Mancini, sweat sheening his bald pate. He glared at Hobson, calm and relaxed.

"Explain your thinking, if you wouldn't mind," smiled Ram.

"He was shot in the back. This man had been wearing a backpack full of heavy camera gear. An arrow would not have penetrated it. It would have been fortunate if the stalker had happened upon him *just* as he took his backpack off."

"Lucky but not impossible. What makes you think our killer was standing over there?" Ram observed.

Hobson nodded.

"True. Well, this man is a bird watcher. He would have been wandering through the bush looking for...photo ops. He saw the parrot nest up there. He took his backpack off and began taking photos. He would have been standing there facing that way. The only spot of decent cover to take those shots would have been the copse."

Ram nodded.

"And the sadism?"

"Coogan said that one of the shots was through the heart. That would have been the kill shot. Well, if this man is such a good shot as to get the heart, with a motionless target taking photos, why did he take two shots?"

The two men shook their heads; Ram was cool behind his shades, while Mancini was wide-eyed. Sweating.

"The first shot was to make him suffer. He would have felt a punch in the back. Pain in the chest. He would have looked down. He saw the arrowhead through his shirt as his lungs filled with blood. His killer wanted him to know what was happening before he died. So he knew he had been murdered. Sounds sadistic to me."

Ram eyed Hobson a moment. With a half-smile, he turned to Mancini.

"Right. Well, thank you, inspector. I'll take it from here."

"Very good, sir. I've tasked Perkins to be your liaison with the locals."

"If you don't mind, I would like Constable Hobson to work with me." Ram gestured to Hobson, who arched an eyebrow behind her glasses.

"I'm afraid Constable Hobson has been confined to a desk for the foreseeable future."

"All the Alfrede, I would like her."

"I bet you would. But Perkins is more than able-"

"I said I would like Constable Hobson, *Inspector*."

Although emphasising the inspector, Ram's voice remained quiet and polite but carried a firmness that brooked no argument.

"But...why?" was all Mancini could think to say.

"Inspector, I am the one they send out to small towns to investigate suspicious deaths. Believe me when I say that in my fifteen years here in Australia, I have worked more than a few. This is one of the rare times the crime scene was properly sealed and evidence was conserved. On top of that, Constable Hobson has already made some very astute observations, formulating some sound hypotheses. Please let me finish." He held his hand up as Mancini was about to interrupt. "Her insight could be invaluable. I can, if you want, go over your head. But I would rather not."

"But she needs to guard the scene." Mancini snapped.

"Good point. My apologies," said Ram with an apologetic nod. Mancini grinned, "Is Perkins here?"

"Perkins," Mancini called.

A wiry sergeant turned from gazing at his reflection in the Land Cruiser's window. He ran across his pointed features, and bulging eyes made him look like a ferret that was being strangled.

"Sir."

Ram stepped forward.

"I am Detective *Superintendent* Ram. Queensland Rural Homicide Unit. Inspector Mancini would like you to watch this crime scene, please." Ram turned and headed up the embankment. "Come on, Hobson. We have work to do. We'll take your car."

Mancini grabbed Ram's arm as he began to walk away.

"You should know, sir, that this lady does not like men. Your chances are slim."

Ram turned, and despite the clear sky and sun, it suddenly felt frosty. No one moved. He looked down at Mancini's hand, which Mancini hesitantly dropped. Ram slowly removed his sunglasses, his dark eyes meeting Mancini's.

"That comment, inspector, tells me much more about you than about Constable Hobson. I suggest we stay out of each other's way from here on."

Hobson looked to Mancini. Mancini's jaw tightened; he leaned in and hissed.

"You're playing a dangerous game, Hobson. One misstep, and you're out. Permanently," he turned and stalked away.

Hobson turned back to Ram, crouched, gazing at the man before him. Hobson moved forward and stopped, staring as she realised he was talking to himself. She edged forward.

"...sorry this has happened to you. You were here, indulging in a hobby when..." he turned to gaze at the tree. "Were you excited by this find? Are you professional?" he looked at the camera. "No. Hobby." He took in the clothes. "You are a professional something. Clothes are a brand. Clean shaven. Hair trimmed. Hands clean. No, a labourer. The gear is not professional-grade, but it is not inexpensive. Not married. Friends? Family?" He looked across at the copse, "But why you? Did you know your killer? If not, why you? Did you owe money? Cheat him? Betray him? Love? Money? Revenge? Or is this just random?"

"Sir?" asked Hobson, not sure if she should respond.

Ram looked up as he reached into his pocket.

"Oh, nothing, constable," he smiled charmingly as he pulled out a large plastic bag. He then worked methodically through the man's pockets, pulling out a wallet, a phone, a notebook and a set of keys. Opening the bag, he dropped the keys in.

"Have you a notepad, constable?" he asked as he opened the wallet.

Hobson hastily patted her pockets and pulled out a small pad and pen. Ram looked at the driver's licence.

"Shoot," she said

"Alfred Cuthbert. 2/32 Arlington Court. There is a teacher's registration card. A bank card. And $50 in cash."

He placed the wallet in the bag and pulled out a mobile phone. He pressed a button.

"We have an emergency number. Clara Cuthbert. Wife? Sister? We will call her."

He read out the number as Hobson wrote it, dropped the phone into the bag, and opened the book.

"Ah, yes. His life list. Very thorough. Dates. Locations. Useful for tracking his movements."

He looked up at Hobson.

"We have some work to do, constable, starting with calling Clara."

Hobson could not help but smile; this was not how she expected today to turn out.

Press releases for this story are based on the following:

https://www.health.qld.gov.au/news-events/doh-media-releases/releases/mask-wearing-in-south-east-queensland-continued-for-another-week2

https://www.health.nsw.gov.au/news/Pages/20210729_02.aspx

All characters in this book are fictitious. Any resemblance between them and real people is purely coincidental.

I hope you enjoyed the read.